DEGREES OF
NAKEDNESS

DEGREES OF
NAKEDNESS

STORIES

LISA MOORE

ANANSI

First published in 1995 by The Mercury Press

This edition published in 2004 by
House of Anansi Press Inc.
110 Spadina Avenue, Suite 801
Toronto, ON, M5V 2K4
Tel. 416-363-4343
Fax 416-363-1017
www.anansi.ca

Distributed in Canada by
Publishers Group Canada
250A Carlton Street
Toronto, ON, M5A 2L1
Tel. 416-934-9900
Toll free order numbers:
Tel. 800-663-5714
Fax 800-565-3770

House of Anansi Press is committed to protecting our natural environment. As part
of our efforts, this book is printed on New Leaf EcoBook 100 paper: it contains
100% post-consumer recycled fibres, is acid-free, and is processed chlorine-free.

08 07 06 05 04   1 2 3 4 5

NATIONAL LIBRARY OF CANADA CATALOGUING IN PUBLICATION DATA

Moore, Lisa Lynne, 1964–
Degrees of nakedness / Lisa Moore. — New ed.

Short stories.
ISBN 0-88784-702-1

I. Title.

PS8576.O61444D44 2004   C813'.54   C2003-906930-3

JAN 2 5 2011

Cover design: Bill Douglas at The Bang
Cover photo: Laura Jane Petelko
Typesetting: Brian Panhuyzen

 Canada Council
for the Arts
Conseil des Arts
du Canada

ONTARIO ARTS COUNCIL
CONSEIL DES ARTS DE L'ONTARIO

*We acknowledge for their financial support of our publishing program the Canada Council
for the Arts, the Ontario Arts Council, and the Government of Canada through
the Book Publishing Industry Development Program (BPIDP).*

Printed and bound in Canada

To Larry Mathews, for encouraging words

Contents

Nipple of Paradise

I expected some epiphany during the birth. Some way to order the material, some profound wisdom. It seems important to document exactly the way it went. In fact I would like to set the whole summer down in point form. Collect it, pin it. The birth, the affair, the postpartum-affair depression. Already I remember the summer in short-hand, distilled, made up of only a hundred or so specific images intermingled; meals, sex, nights on the fire escape, hours in the office, the birth, the affair. And by next summer I won't even remember it that clearly. But for now it has reached the half-dissolved stage, the separate gestures of the summer exaggerated like the colour in Polaroid photographs.

After I found out that Cy had slept with Marie I sat on the fire escape with my foot on the railing, and a spider crawled over my foot, my toes tensed, each toe stretching away from the others. I could feel the spider make its web, lacing my toes together. It struck me that I had never felt anything so sharply before. That's how a story should work. Like that Chinese ribbon dance. They turn off the lights so you can't see the dancer. All you see are two long fluorescent ribbons, drawing in the dark, like the strokes of that summer. Or that guy Volker we met in Germany, did drawings with a pen flashlight inside a cave. A photographer Volker knew shot them with fast film. Volker was a shadow but he drew the outlines of men and women embracing. He said it took incredible concentration because he had only ten seconds to make the drawing. The result was a fury of limbs locked through each other, the lines themselves seared onto the walls of a cave, the condensation glittering like sweat.

Example: Hannah, Cy's daughter, in her satin ballet costume, black with red sequins, lime green tulle, dragging herself up the staircase, howling like a wolf, "I got no one to play with, I got no one to play with," hand over hand on the banister while the sky blisters with rain, while Cy and I make love in the bathroom. He's soaking in this chemical blue bubble bath Hannah bought him for Christmas the first year I met him. It comes out of a plastic bottle shaped like a Havana nightclub dancer. The woman's hat, a mountain of bananas, unscrews, and although the bubbles are turquoise, the bathroom stinks of synthetic bananas. We try to make love first on the side of the tub but it's slippery from the steam, then on the toilet, and then one foot on the radiator, hiked up on the sink so I can see my own sunburnt face in the antique mirror we found in an abandoned house around the bay. The mirror is watery, my face wobbled with laughter because the position is so ridiculous, my legs bound by the pink maternity overalls wrapped around my knees and Hannah banging now on the bathroom door. Cy comes, and then both of us are completely still, him hugging me from behind. We look at each other's faces in the mirror. His hand is on my belly and the baby kicks so hard that both our eyes widen at the same time. We answer Hannah in unison, "Just a second." I haul up my overalls while Cy opens the door. "Jeez," says Hannah and sits on the toilet to pee.

After the baby was born, and I was still drugged, I thought I felt her move again, inside me. I guess it was like when someone feels an itch in a missing limb. It was only a ghost of the way she felt inside me, and already I was forgetting what it had felt like to have her flutter in there, as if a million years had passed.

I didn't really get the chance to read very much birthing literature. I'd collected it, seen a film of an Australian woman who gave birth in her own living room. Her next-door neighbour dropped over, made himself a cup of tea and ended up holding the mirror for her, between her legs. She wore an old T-shirt and moaned in an Australian accent. The baby was blue when it came out. Cy gritted his teeth while he watched.

Our Bodies, Ourselves says that some male partners seek other sexual partners during the pregnancy. "You wouldn't do that, would you, Cy?"

We only got to one of the pre-natal classes. It happened to be the one on "Things that can go wrong." The nurse started off by assuring everyone that in most cases nothing goes wrong, but that we had to go through this anyhow, just in case. She showed the suction cups the doctors sometimes use during natural births. They had pink cups and blue cups, the nurse told us, ". . . but as sure as shooting, if you used the pink cup you'd get a boy and vice versa. The funny thing about these cups is they seem to go in and out of fashion. You might notice a certain doctor using them for a couple of months and then it seems the cups stay in the cupboard for six months and nobody uses them. They don't hurt the baby, of course, except they do sometimes come out with cone-shaped heads when the doctor uses the suction cups. In fact you have to be careful after you have the baby that you lay him on different sides every time you lay him down, otherwise his head will go flat. Actually, there's a little community up the southern shore that's into head sculpting. All of them have heads as flat as frying pans on one side." And she snorted, "No, that's only a joke."

She said the last time she brought the forceps to a lecture one of the dads got upset, so this time she was only bringing a diagram. She held up the diagram for a moment without comment and then slid it behind the next diagram which was of a baby whose head was too big to fit through the pelvic hole. At the end of the session she got everyone to lie down on a mat and she played a relaxing tape. "Come on, now, dads, don't be shy, down on the mats with the moms." She turned the lights off so the room was black. Cy and I lay down on a gym mat and listened while a sultry female voice told us our toes, ankles, knees, hip joints and so on up the body were feeling feather light, as if all the tension of the day was leaving our bodies in waves. There was a soundtrack of waves and sitar music in the background. Beside me I could feel Cy's shoulder shuddering in a silent fit of giggles.

I guess I should describe the woman Cy slept with, Marie. She was beautiful and unemployed all summer. Thick curly black hair, long suntanned legs. She didn't believe in marriage. Not only did she never plan to marry but she didn't acknowledge anyone else's. She had a Marxist approach to the whole thing. "Love isn't a commodity. A wife is a whore, only real whores are more honest about it and have more fun. Marriage is a business contract whereby women sell men exclusive sex rights, allowing the male to control the means of reproduction in exchange for financial security. Romantic love is a corrupt notion that leads ultimately to death by excruciating boredom. Besides, I can't help how I feel about Cy." And she winked at me.

Marie, the night I found out they had slept together: Cy has invited her to supper. She brings us chocolates wrapped in gold foil with miniature Rembrandt paintings printed on it. Rembrandt's fat creamy wife. Cy is excited about the wrappers because he's working on a thesis for an Art History degree. He collects everybody's wrappers and begs Marie to eat the last chocolate. She laughs and tosses it at his chest. It bounces off and nearly hits the baby rocking in her cradle beside Cy's chair.

The Party: we are having fondue. Cy spills the starter fluid and when he lights it the fondue pot bursts into flames. The table is full of flammable things we somehow hadn't noticed before: dishtowels, the bottle of starter fluid, a yellow Styrofoam duck that Hannah's art teacher made for parents who volunteered to wear it on their heads for a swim-a-thon for cancer. Cy and I are screaming at each other. Hannah comes into the kitchen and we both scream, "Get out of the kitchen" in unison. Marie promptly throws a dishtowel on the fondue pot. There are a few clouds of black smoke. She lifts the towel off, magician-like, and there are no more flames. We stare at the pot for a few seconds and the flames burst back to life. The heat reaches the neck of the duck, melting it so the duck's beak opens angrily. Marie puts the cloth back on the pot and the fire goes out. Later in the evening, everybody is drunk and raucous except me, because I'm still pregnant. We have eaten all evening, asparagus, carrots, broccoli dipped in hot wine cheese fondue, chunks of pumpernickel. Someone has suggested I wear the Styrofoam duck on my head throughout the evening. I protested but everyone booed me. I don't want to seem excruciatingly boring, so I wear it. Marie picks up an empty wine bottle and blows into it. It sounds eerie and hollow and for a minute it sobers everyone. Suddenly Marie's chair collapses beneath her. In slow motion she reaches both her arms out to Cy. Their fingers grip for a second and she hits the floor. She is laughing so hard she's in tears.

The Birth: She came a month and a half early. A thirty-weeker as they call them in the neo-natal nursery. It was a caesarean. We arrived at the hospital at one in the morning and entered the case room. The nurses' station glowed like a spaceship because the lights in the hall were dimmed. The nurse looked at me with a raised eyebrow as if my street clothes were a faux pas. They took Cy and me to a room and smeared jelly over my belly and hooked me to monitors. The baby's heart rate was scratched on a spewing paper in fine red ink. The doctor came and said I should be operated on right away but he had two caesareans ahead of me.

"Each of them will take a half hour or so and then we'll do you." They were back in exactly one hour. In the delivery room, everyone was masked and wearing paper hats covered with mauve and blue flowers. A giant convex mirror hung from the ceiling, but I had to be hunched up in a fetal position. The epidural was like freezing water dribbling down my spine. They put a blue curtain across my chest and gathered around the table which was uncomfortably narrow. The anaesthetist was at my head. He sat next to a large box with dials and monitors. There was a tube in my back in case something went wrong and he had to administer more anaesthetic. Somebody was shaving my pubic hair.

"How's that?"

"He likes it lower than that."

"Where's Cy?" I asked.

"We'll let Cy in when we're ready," the anaesthetist said.

When Cy came in he was wearing a mauve and blue flowered cap also. He kneeled next to me, holding my hand, smoothing my hair. "I can still feel my toes," I said.

"It's not your toes we're operating on," said the anaesthetist. "You will feel sensation, you'll feel them cutting you, but no pain."

I heard them pull the tray of instruments across the floor. Suddenly I was swept with fear and just as suddenly it was gone. I felt the knife pressing across my belly. Cy began to smooth my hair with more vigour until his stroke became so vigorous I had to stop him. There was a sucking noise.

"That was your water breaking," said someone behind the curtain. The anaesthetist looked over the curtain,

"Black hair," he said. "It's a girl."

"Is she healthy?" I asked.

"Appears to be."

The sense of relief was absolute. I had planned to write about the birth as soon as I found out I was pregnant. I figured the epiphany would come then, that I would be wiser at that moment, the moment of birth. But I was dumbfounded. It's taken me two months to find that word dumbfounded but it struck me walking down the street yesterday. For the ten days I was in hospital I didn't write a word. Not a letter or thank-you note. It took us a month and a half to figure out a name for her. I couldn't find any significance, the birth wasn't a symbol or metaphor, it just happened, a clean thing, a thing unto itself, a pure wordless thing. I was struck dumb.

They lay her on my chest. Her head was small as a fist. Green guck of some sort all over her hair. The anaesthetist put his hand over her closed eyes to block the light so she would open them. They were black and wet like those of a newborn kitten. We held her there while they sewed me up. Cy said he saw her in the mirror first, being passed from hand to hand. Then all the doctors shook Cy's hand, congratulating him.

The nurses in the neo-natal unit said Cy was the best father they'd seen. They said, "She'll have him wrapped around her little finger."

There were four other women besides me at the breast feeding class they offer in the hospital. We all had self-righteous expressions. We had heard that only thirty percent of Newfoundland women breast feed. The nurse speaks without stopping for breath, "Now, girls, some of the dads might be uncomfortable with the breast feeding at first, but sure that's only natural. You'll find that when you climax while you're having sex you'll probably be squirting milk all over him. Just keep a towel handy, that's all, and don't worry about the public. Nobody cares unless you're in the mall and you strip off down to the waist. Now, you know yourself, girls, you have to use a little common sense and girls, if you're going to a cocktail party, double pad, because I'm telling you now, once you get a drop of wine in you it's going to be like Churchill Falls and you're going to have to go in the bathroom and wring out your cocktail dress."

The nurse puts on an instructional video in which a fifty-year-old woman holds a stuffed doll to her blouse in the various different breast feeding positions. She holds it under one arm, the legs kicking behind. White letters appear on the screen: Football position. Then the video shows actual mothers, who look worn out, still in hospital johnny coats, close-ups on their breasts, which are swollen, blue-veined and mountainous next to the newborn babies. Breast feeding is a skill, the narrator tells us.

My baby was too small to suck from my nipple so we had to feed her pumped breast milk from a bottle. I had to pump every night. Fit the plastic cone over my swollen, rock-hard breast and flick the little lever that starts the pump. I've seen the pump that we use to get water from the well. This pump was the same size. A two thousand dollar machine. It makes a loud grinding noise. After three days I thought I was bonding with it. Cy sat with me while my milk squirted into the attached cup. I showed him the four ounce mark. "Look how much I got."

"That's great, Donna."

In the long exhausted week after she was born, we went to the hospital cafeteria so Cy could smoke. It's a small room with a few tables, tinfoil ashtrays, lit mostly by the lights in the snack machines. There were meals of macaroni and soup that could be heated in the microwave, all displayed in racks that rotated when you pushed a button. At ten at night we had the cafeteria to ourselves, except for a nurse who came in with a flattened piece of shiny paper. She put it in the microwave and watched it as if it were a TV, pulling over a rickety chair and resting her elbows on her knees, chin in hand. The microwave choked into action, the inside lit up and a red light played on the package until it expanded with bursting popcorn kernels into a round smooth ball that split in a line up the centre. When she left, Cy reached into the pocket of his coat and pulled out a small box.

"I got you something."

It was a bottle of moisturizing cream. I had run out but I'd told Cy not to get any because we couldn't afford it. Tears came to my eyes.

Cy said, "Ah, for Jesus' sake, Donna."

"Well, I'm tired, Cy, I'm just plain tired."

I guess it was somewhere during that week he slept with Marie. I found out because of the baby monitor. We got this monitor, you put one piece in the baby's cradle and the other you carry around with you. It's so sensitive you can hear the baby breathe or hiccup. It took a little getting used to. Sometimes it would pick up the voices of children playing on the street, the sound garbled and static as if the baby had been invaded by aliens who were using her as a vehicle to relay a message. Once, at midnight, Cy and I were sitting at the living room table, having a cup of coffee, watching the couples coming up from the Ship Inn, when there was a loud crash over the monitor. Both of us froze for a second and then ran up the stairs, two at a time. In her room, everything was still. The bassinet was in the centre of the table where we had left it. Cy looked out the window. Somebody on the street had slammed a car door.

The night Marie came over for supper Cy took her up to the bedroom to see the baby. He forgot the monitor was on.

He said, "Listen, Marie, what happened, if Donna knew about it, it would really hurt her, I mean I really had a good time, but I think it was a sort of solitary thing."

His voice was soft and without static. It was as if he were standing behind me, telling me about it. I went out on the fire escape with my cup of coffee, put my feet up on the banister.

I had been so weak the whole time I was in hospital. The baby was the smallest baby in the neo-natal nursery. I was okay when Cy was with me, but when I had to go into the nursery by myself I was convinced they were going to tell me something terrible. They have huge stainless steel sinks with digital clocks that tell you how many seconds you've been scrubbing. While I washed up to the elbow, I would convince myself not to start crying. Once I went in, and they said, "Now, Mrs. Sheppard, I better tell you this before you see your baby, there's nothing to worry about, but she stopped breathing for a minute or so. That's common with premature babies, one of the nurses noticed she was a little dusky-coloured and picked her up and she was fine. But we've got a monitor on her now and I just wanted to mention it to you before you saw her, so you'd know there was nothing to worry about."

I phoned Cy and he said he'd be up right away. I stood in the bathroom of my hospital room looking in the mirror, smoothing moisturizing cream over my face. When Cy got there he held me in his arms for a long time. When visiting hours were over, he went home and phoned me. They had wheeled a patient into my room who had just given birth, so I couldn't talk, I could only listen.

Cy read to me from a history book about Christopher Columbus. Columbus wrote to Ferdinand that he had sighted cyclops and mermaids who were not as beautiful as previously reported, in fact quite mannish. They believed back then that the garden of Paradise was on Earth. That the world was pear-shaped, and the garden of Eden a protuberance on the top, like a woman's nipple. When Columbus found South America, he knew he had come to land because fresh water was mixing with sea water and whales played there. He thought that fresh water flowed from the nipple of Paradise. When I woke up, the telephone receiver was buzzing the dial tone in my ear.

Out on the fire escape, the fog coming up from the harbour penetrated my clothes and a spider crawled over my foot. Cy came out, and I said to him, "Cy, how do I know you won't leave me?"

He said, "You don't know, Donna. I love you fiercely right now, that's the best I can offer."

I thought about that artist, Volker, we'd visited in Germany. He had taken Cy and me into his painting studio and showed us paintings for two hours. Suddenly, he said, "Come here, Cyril, I will show you something." He grabbed Cy's thumb and dipped it into a can of gold pigment, powdered gold. Cy held up his gilded thumb. It looked as if a fragment of an ancient statue were somehow attached to Cy's living hand. It made me think of Hansel and Gretel, how the witch said, Show me your thumb so I can see if you're fattened up, and Hansel held out a chicken bone. Buying precious time. It made me think that love is made of isolated flashes and they are what we crave. It was getting dark outside Volker's studio and Cy's thumb glowed like something precious, timeless.

Sea Urchin

We were alone on the island, at your parents' cottage. Oil lamps at night, the darkness collapsing like a tent. The day before I left, during supper, my mother and I couldn't look each other in the eye. I watched her try to jerk a speared beet off her fork. A hard cube, brilliant magenta drops splatting the white plate. Shortly after my father died I left her to go to art school. I had been home two weeks and I was leaving again for Georgian Bay. But she let me go.

An island in Georgian Bay. Forty-five minutes in a speedboat away from the next community. Hundreds of islands. We flew stand-by from Newfoundland and in between flights I went into the airport washroom and stood looking at my face. Looking to see if I was pretty. Mesmerized. Was I pretty at all? When I came out we had missed the connecting flight.

What were you doing? you said. What were you doing in the bathroom?

You were chopping wood. I drank six beers, fast, then ate a bowl of popcorn coated with half a block of melted cheddar. I stumbled out of the cottage. Fell onto the sand at the beach and screamed your name. Over and over. It was just us on the island. Nude half the time. Shouting your name, sending it lurching through the pines.

You took me to a cliff and told me to jump. It was a long way down. I took off my glasses, and handed them to you. The water was a hard bed of shiny dimes. It hurt the bottoms of my feet. Under the surface, the cliff was gouged away, a dark mouth. I imagined it was dense with eels.

My father died just before I met you. His hair had turned grey when he was about your age, eighteen. It had been blondish-red before that, he told me. All the photographs of him before eighteen are hand-tinted, so I don't know what shade of red, but he had the complexion of a redhead. He sunburned easily and when he drank or became emotional, his skin would break out in red blotches, quickly, like the wind blowing a field of poppies all in the same direction. I imagine his hair turning grey overnight. He might have gotten out of bed, looked in the mirror and been startled out of his wits. Wondered what it could possibly mean. Maybe I imagine that his hair turned grey overnight rather than gradually, because he died overnight, without any symptom or warning.

My father's brother, Uncle Lloyd, died this year.

My mother and I gripped each other in the parking lot of the funeral home. It was icy and for several minutes we couldn't gain any ground. We just clung to each other. She said, Why would a man like Lloyd get to live so much longer than your father?

There was one wreath from the Salvation Army on the coffin. The metal trees with shelves for flowers at the head and foot were empty. A man slept in the armchair. The bottoms of his brown creased pants were salt crusted, his legs crossed. He wore sneakers, one of the Velcro flaps hanging loose, and one foot nodding, stroking time.

Mom and I went close to the casket. Uncle Lloyd didn't look the way I remembered him. I thought I'd see my father's face, because the brothers all looked alike, but I was disappointed. There was nothing familiar. His nose was slightly squashed to one side, as if they'd closed the lid on it. I checked inside the satin roof to see if there might be a smudge of face powder, but the frills were clean and white. I almost touched the nose to push it back into place. Lloyd's eyelashes were light and in this way, at least, he resembled my father. For an instant I was overcome by the belief that a nerve in his eyelid had twitched.

The last time I saw Lloyd was in Barbados, when I was a child. He'd come on vacation with us. That was before he'd begun drinking. Dad stepped on a sea urchin. The long needles were driven deep into his foot, touching bone. They cracked off. Within seconds, his foot was swollen and red. A janitor at the hospital told my father the only cure was to pour heated wax over the foot. That would draw the needles out. He propped his leg on a pillow, both hands gripping his shin. Lloyd wiped the sand from Dad's foot and spread the melted wax with a piece of cardboard. I don't know where my mother was. Dad's face twisted with pain. The heat of the wax drew the inch-long needles out. The smell of salt water and hot paraffin. I remembered this when Mom called to tell me Lloyd had died. My father has been dead eleven years and I'm still discovering lost pieces of him.

You're unravelling fast, too. First love. When you cross my mind you're like a composite drawing a police artist makes from the testimony of witnesses. I rarely think of you.

Your mother left condoms in a pile on your bed next to your airline ticket. A few pamphlets.

Your mother and father were brand new for me. For one thing, the house you lived in was rented. Property was bourgeois, your mother said. They were joking, but they were the only parents I knew who didn't own their house or want to. They had art. Blue wine goblets, antiques. You could see a line down the side of the glass where two halves of the mould had been joined, but each glass was different. Wine at supper. Home-made salad dressing instead of Kraft.

Once I saw your mother eat raw hamburger with a raw egg. The fork prying the fibres of cold pink meat, a peach fuzz of congealed fat, burst yolk. Popping it in her mouth.

Your father wore a custard-coloured suit. A few shades lighter than custard. When I was nine I went with my father to shop for a suit. He wanted grey but I was to choose the shade. There were thousands of suits on the wall in two rows, one beneath the other, each suit a slightly lighter shade of grey than the one next to it.

At art school there was a drawing exercise to get as many shades out of an HB pencil as you could. Only one of the grey suits was exquisite. Dad tried on the one I chose. He stood facing the mirror, then in three-quarter profile, smoothed his hands down the front. Touched the bottom edge of the jacket. He asked me if I was sure. After a moment he asked me again. Then he bought the suit with a large wad of money. It was the most money I had ever seen spent in one place. His only suit. He was buried in it. And there was your father, in something lighter than custard.

If you've never experienced grief you don't recognize it. When I met you I was full of grief. During an art history class we saw a slide of a sculpture, *The Ecstasy of Saint Theresa*. A woman arched as in orgasm, pierced with thousands of arrows. I closed my eyes and imagined my whole body covered with tiny needles, an ocean current making them sway gently, a sweet numbing pain.

I took an interest in astral projection. I tried. It was hot and I lay on the army cot in the dormitory with my fists clenched. I tried to float off the bed. I believed in God until my father died.

And I believed my body was the temple of God. This didn't mean I couldn't have sex until I was married, but that as soon as I was penetrated I'd be spiritually sewn to that man forever. Fated to him. If we had sex I'd be fated to you.

I slept. Sleep was like oxygen. I couldn't quite get enough to fill my lungs. At six in the evening I'd make excuses to go to my room. Ten minutes later I'd be asleep with my clothes on.

I'd wake up late for school. I had hallucinations while I slept. I'd sit up and pinch myself as hard as I could. In the morning there'd be small bruises, but even while pinching I'd see the iron bars of the radiator melt at the bottom like knee socks that had fallen around the ankles, or the sky, filled with stars, force itself through the open window, float over the cot until I was looking up into the cloudy universe, terrified.

I was volunteering at the women's penitentiary, teaching art to one student who had attacked her sister with a hammer, causing brain damage. She was so blind her nose touched the paper while she drew and it would sometimes be daubed with paint. She always painted the same picture, Christ with his arms spread, in a white robe, on the far side of a navy river. Her bleary eyes and the blue paint on her nose made me think she was trying to dive into the river, reach Christ.

She did the same painting over and over until her migraine made her stop. I chattered all the while she painted. What do you say to someone who believes that when the guards turn off the light in her cell she is visited by a bulldog with the face of a man and the tongue of a snake?

I told her about the night sky visiting me. She lined the paintings edge to edge to edge until I began to think it was a message for me. Was it my father on the other side of the river trying to cross? Arms open to me. Or was it me? Was it me unable to cross to myself?

One day I left a pencil behind and she gouged it into her arm, ripping open the vein.

You didn't talk much. On weekends, or at night, I'd make you hitch-hike to an empty part of the highway with me. The highway cut through the darkness. Sometimes all we could see was the yellow line. Every so often the pavement would vibrate through the rubber soles of our sneakers and the headlights from transport trucks came up from behind us. The lights swiped like giant paws over the trees and boulders until they overtook us and we fell back into darkness.

I just talked and shouted and did cartwheels and the cancan with my parka open. I did chorus kicks all the way down the empty highway. I shrieked the lyrics from old musicals; *I got plenty of nothin' and nothin's plenty for me.* The hills climbed up on either side of us. Rain fell off the massive sky like the faces of buildings in an earthquake.

It's possible to imagine you have completely forgotten me.

You were honest. That was a point with you. I've been with men who believe they're honest, but the truth loses its shape around them. I prefer them. You never said you loved me, even when I begged you.

Please say you love me just once. Please, please, please, please, I'll devote my whole life to you, I'll do anything. I was holding onto the hem of your jeans. We were in the echoey stairwell. I was flat on my belly, on the stairs, being dragged with each step you took, breathless with laughter. You drawing one leg up, then the other, pulling yourself up by the railing. In danger of losing your pants. Please say it, just say it for Christ's sake.

I'm trying to imagine what it must have felt like to be the

object of that much devotion. You were stern, that was your policy. In the face of obsession, be stern.

I was in a high school play the night my father died. I stood on a ladder. I was Voice Number Three. I talked about spring coming, and wore a feather boa dyed orange. I changed a Styrofoam painting of autumn leaves on a plywood tree for a Styrofoam painting of green ones. Mom was waiting in the wings. She said I'd have to come right away, Dad was sick.

That night the nurse told us he would die. A heart attack. It seemed to me an easy thing to fix. There must be some kind of syringe to suck the blood back into the heart so it can pump again, some surgery. I explained this to the nurse. I had an image of the heart as one of those hard plastic models stuck on a steel spike in the science lab. But a heart, in fact, must be like tissue paper, must come apart when it's not pumping, must dissolve. He had wires attached to little white circles attached to his chest. He looked very tidy, not soaked in blood at all.

The next day I wanted to go to school as though nothing had happened. My mother didn't stop me. In school there was a surprise party for a teacher who was having a baby. Everybody chipped in on the present. She held it up, tissue paper over the sides of the box. She made a joke and everybody laughed uproariously, the excitement of a free period. Miss, Miss, Miss, and over the noise of my own laughter she mouthed the words, How's your father? and I mouthed back, Dead.

Her shock hit me in the stomach. The bell rang and everyone jumped up to leave. In the corridor I leaned against the wall, unable to hold myself up.

We had sex outdoors a lot for lack of any other location, living as we were in student dorms, no boys on the girls' floor, and vice versa. Once in the mud and yellow leaves, criss-crossing black branches above us, a crude basket that would catch us if we fell into the sky. The smell of mud. You had a moustache. Not a very full one, mousy, the separate hairs bending like drawn bows against my lips. A wallet with a Velcro hasp, a condom in the billfold. Once we had sex beside a river in the middle of a snowstorm, the water churning brown, headlights sweeping over us, wind blasting, my breasts and stomach exposed to the falling snow. You ripped the Velcro with your lips, the body of the wallet tucked between your chin and shoulder.

Later, after we'd gotten an apartment of our own, and you decided it wasn't working, you refused to sleep with me. Once I tried to force you, burst into the spare room while you were in bed, straddling you, kissing you, trying to get at your belt. We struggled and you pushed me off, dragged me to the window and ripped my shirt open. Pressed me against the window, half naked. Two empty parking lots and the fire station. Nobody saw. Once while I was asleep you came into our room and kissed me, kissed my cheeks, kissed my neck, and when I was drawn awake, when I put my arms around your neck, you left the room. You couldn't explain it, the leaving, except to say if we didn't break up we would stay together forever.

This is the sad thing about loving. It's a skill, like working up a clay pot on a wheel. As though the form is slipping to life by itself, the hands slicked with juicy mud are doing all they can to contain it. Just the tiniest squeezing of muscles in the hands keeps the pot perfect. It's such a shock to throw a pot for the first time and see how unsimple it is, to have it skew, deform and collapse in seconds, against what you expect.

I was terrified of dying suddenly, like my father. My skin was a mess. I burst into hysterical laughter for no reason, laughed until I was in tears. I'm only remembering what I did, because I can't remember how I felt.

When I was thirteen I developed an ovarian cyst. It was removed and turned out to be benign. After the doctor's appointment when the cyst was diagnosed, my mother and I stopped at my father's office. My father said, How's it going? and my mother said, Our little girl isn't having a very good day.

At that moment, having to tell my father I was going to be operated on made me feel infinitely sad for myself, and for him. I felt I was letting him down. I opened my mouth to say something but I couldn't. My father pressed my face into his chest so hard I could feel the button of his shirt digging into my forehead. My mother told him, and when I looked up at him he was smiling as if an operation wasn't such a bad thing. But his face had broken out in soft red blotches.

After the operation, when I was recovering, my father cooked me a fresh trout. He had taken the green canoe out on the lake before sunrise, the water so still the leaping trout startled him. He made twists of lemon and bought some parsley sprigs to decorate it. But on the way through the screen door he dropped the plate. Broken splinters of china covered the fish. My mother told me about it later. She said he cried. For a long time I associated his crying with his death, rather than my illness. I remembered not myself in the hospital, but him and the nurse telling me he would die by morning. As he was coming through the screen door, he must have realized he would be leaving me, how hurt I would be, how irreparable it was, and the shock of it made him drop the plate.

I dreamt last night that Mom and I were sitting naked on my bedroom floor. She had a tin filled with beeswax or shoe polish. She said if I smeared the stuff in my vagina it would make me pregnant. This way I could avoid the risk of having the father die after the child was born. There'd never be a father to die. My child wouldn't have anything to lose. I had agreed to get pregnant this way, but at the last minute I was backing out. I knew I wanted my child to have a father, no matter how much pain it would cause to lose him.

The first time you kissed me, the whole town was buried in snow. Some drifts went to the tops of the telephone poles. It was like walking on the moon. Everything curved, everything buried, deceptive, muted. We were coming back from a movie and you leaned me against the orange bricks of the dorm. A drift came to our waists and snow blew off the lip of it, swirled around us, hissing on the back of your nylon parka.

You sucked my tongue. Our hands were linked loosely, two or three fingers twined. It was as though you were pulling my whole self, all the pain from my father's death, all the loneliness of being separated from my mother, all my loud babbling, siphoning it up through my body into my tongue, and taking it into your mouth, until my tongue felt swollen. Until I wasn't even thinking of who you were any more. Just the sucking that seemed to be drawing out the sadness. Heat, like the needles being drawn from my father's foot with melted wax. I was trembling. When you stopped kissing me I had nothing to say. My lips cracked when I smiled. I ran my tongue over them and they stung.

Do you remember Joyce, my roommate in the dorm? She slept on the other side of a half-wall that divided the room. She told me when I first met her that she was asthmatic, and showed me where she kept her respirator. I woke one night to the sound of choked spasmodic breathing. I thought she was dying. I filled up with that quicksand of sleep and fear, so heavy I couldn't move, not even my mouth, to scream for help, but in that same second I had flung off the sheets and jumped out of bed, my skin already clammy, and I called her name.

Two things went through my head simultaneously. Death was coming again, and it had missed me. It had skipped over my bed because I was waiting for it; even in my sleep I had outwitted it. Not only that but I would save Joyce from it too. The second thing came in the voice of a nun who taught me math in grade eleven and failed me. A nun with pasty skin, someone I hated. But she had showed up at my father's funeral and gripped my shoulders so tightly it hurt, and that pain seemed to keep me from passing out. Her voice came into my head at that exact moment and said, Don't take another step, she's having sex.

Then a male voice said, Your roommate.

Joyce said, She's asleep, she talks in her sleep, she's always yelling stuff.

It took me a full two minutes to get back in the bed without a creak. Then I lay there listening. Frightened they would figure out I was awake, my heart pounding so hard I felt short of breath, and at the same time conscious that I had to make my breath sound deep, the way it is when you're asleep. The more I tried to breathe evenly, the more erratic my breathing, until I had the bed sheet stuffed in my mouth. It was the first time I had ever heard what sex sounds like, the bed creaking, the moans. It stopped suddenly and Joyce asked him to pass her a Kleenex off the desk. I fell asleep deeply, for the first time since my father died, without dreams, as if I had been given an injection.

Wisdom Teeth

They call it a state of emergency. White dervishes scour Stephenville, the blue arm of the plough impotently slashes through the snow. In St. John's where my mother is, the wires are frozen with sleet and the electricity is out. She's in the plaid chair, I know, one emergency candle and a flashing drink of rye.

She's thinking of Barbados. She's thinking of a warm night when she wears a chiffon dress that floats around her, first in the breeze, and then like a flower opening in the swimming pool, swaying its petals. She's wearing a spaghetti strainer on her head and singing into a wooden spoon, "Until the twelfth of never and that's a long time." My father holds a cigarette between his index finger and thumb. He's wearing a floppy hat with peace signs and dancing the flamenco, singing, "Ya ta ta" under his breath.

My mother is thinking of making love while monkeys dash

coconut shells at the corrugated tin roof. Outside chunks of icicles fall from the eaves.

I'm in Stephenville, at the community college. Herpes capital of Newfoundland, the Heavy Equipment guys say. Stephenville has one traffic light, a penitentiary, a bar called the El Dorado, and a long beach with round stones, driftwood and pink tampon applicators.

I'm a Trojan woman that summer. We do it outdoors on the war memorial. The stage is lit with torches. Helen is this woman from New York and that annoys the girls from Beauty Culture. She comes out in a see-through negligee from Woolco. All the Heavy Equipment guys are there, and Bartending, Cooking, Community Studies and Travel Counselling. Nobody catcalls. The other Trojan women and I writhe in the background.

In September the town is fog-soaked and since all the barracks look identical, I get lost. Sometimes I end up at the airport landing strip with the sound of a plane bearing down on me, but from what direction? I spend two nights a week at the movie theatre watching Chuck Norris or David Carradine. Some nights I'm the only one there.

I fall in love with my art teacher because he tells me to paint with my whole arm. He lets me ride in his truck with him on the abandoned airstrip, his Newfoundland dog loping beside us. The windows of the hangar flash morse code. He listens while I talk about Mother Teresa. I love him so much I stutter every time I speak to him. Then I meet his wife and just love him in an uncomplicated way, which is a relief.

That was the first time I left my mother. Now I'm in Toronto. I'm here with Mike, my husband, a graduate student. I followed him here. I have to explain that to everyone I meet, except Darlene. Darlene doesn't know what she's doing here either. Besides, she doesn't judge me, or if she does she keeps it to herself. I'm in a lot of pain because my wisdom teeth are growing in.

Darlene is on her way to Japan to teach businessmen how to speak English. She's just finished her Master's in Art Education. She's accomplished. We walk through Chinatown together without saying much to each other. We look at strange vegetables. She says, unfolding an unwieldy map, "I had a dream I'm pregnant in a kitchen and my hands are magnetic. Forks and knives fly out of the drawers and my hands become so heavy with cutlery I can't lift them."

I say, "A woman on Dundas was stabbed to death with an ice pick by her husband."

Darlene is waiting for her Japanese visa. It could take two weeks. We both apply for jobs at the Royal Ontario Museum. Phone salespersons, membership promotion. The guy phones me for an interview. His voice is like caramel. Almost seductively he says, "So, Jill, what makes you think you've got what it takes?"

I meet Darlene in Stephenville. She's sixteen. She wears black lipstick, black leather skirts and gogo boots that go all the way up to her thighs. She convinces me to go to the El Dorado. The band is from Banff. We go early because there's no one on the door then to check I.D. I'm wearing Darlene's cowboy boots, a black peasant skirt and a gold headband. A guy comes over and offers to buy us a drink. Darlene says, "I'd rather drink hemlock." The guy says, "What's wrong with your friend?" When he leaves I say, "Darlene, he was only trying to be nice." She slits her eyes at me. The disco ball begins its slow revolutions, eggs of light spray one wall, then the other, and then Darlene's cheekbones and hands. She is seeing Harry, who is in the pen for dealing hash. They let him out to go to Art class but he wants to transfer to Heavy Equipment. Darlene memorizes the whole air-brake manual so she can quiz him. She tells me he sneaks hash into jail, wrapped in a condom stuck up his bum. Harry doesn't like me. He says I look like too much of a virgin. But it's Friday and Harry's in for the evening.

On stage the light show starts and they have dry ice. The taped music dies a groggy death; someone pulls the plug. Rich leaps onto stage. He wears jeans and a red T-shirt with a black sickle. The T-shirt has been torn from the neck to reveal a chest of golden hair. He struts across the floor swinging the microphone in circles near the amps so that it makes a zoom zoom sound. Everyone squeezes onto the dance floor and rocks to this sound. Rich tucks the mike between his legs and claps his hands over his head. People clap their hands over their heads. Rich bends double and screams into the mike, "All right!"

The drummer smashes the cymbals.

"Yeah," screams Rich.

"Uh huh," answers the crowd.

Darlene and I dance together. Darlene has her eyes closed,

she barely moves, her fingers stretch and relax with the beat. I twist and gyrate. I'm homesick. The telephone lines are out in St. John's where my mother is. This snow storm has gone on for three days, and it's getting more violent by the hour.

Mike and I start hunting for an apartment in Toronto. The heat exhausts us. One super says, "Youse don't have no pets, youse don't have no parking, youse pay heat, weese pay hydro. Youse fill out these forms and leave 'em face down."

I write, "Waitress, presently unemployed, no bank account at present, spouse: student." The woman beside me writes, "Art Director, Telemedia Corporation." I push back the petals of my torn gum with my tongue and unwrap the tinfoil from my two-twenty-twos.

I wake up crying that night because I've bitten my own cheek. It's infected and swollen. My crying wakes Mike.

"I've bitten my own cheek, I have to call my mother."

"It's two in the morning, she has to work, can't you call her later?"

"Well, I'd just like her to know."

"Come on, Jill, get back in bed."

"I bit my own cheek."

My mother takes risks. She falls down a well when she's nine. When her father hauls her out, her hair stands out from her head like a halo with the pieces of cardboard and straw that someone has dared her to stand on. She holds a rope a second too long while water-skiing and smacks into the wharf. She opens too early from a double somersault, tearing the skin of her shins against the diving board. Ribbons of blood twirl around her in the water like a maypole. She paints the house in her underwear high on a scaffold so when the electrician comes she has to hobble across a wobbly two-by-four in her black lace bra.

I say to her late at night, "You won't catch me loving someone that much, that hard. I'm going to have my own bank account. I'll be a single mother. Nobody's leaving me for another woman and nobody's going to die on me. That's for sure."

She says, "You don't know what you're missing."

End of first set. Dry ice dissolves, taped music lurches back to life. Rich is coming in our direction. He sits down with us. "You like the music." It's not a question. He's talking to me, not Darlene.

"Oh, yeah, you guys are great, you're really alive."

Darlene excuses herself.

His eyes slide down my body, and back up. He moves a handful of hair over my shoulder, touching my neck with his finger.

"You want to dance?"

Before he goes back on stage he chucks me gently under the chin. "You going to stay around?"

"Sure, Rich."

Rich takes me back to the band apartment, over the Lick a Chick take-out. There's a party going on but he takes me directly to the bedroom. The drummer is in bed.

"Frankie, out," says Rich, jerking his head at me.

"Jesus," says Frankie and throws off the sheets. He's wearing leopard-skin briefs, polyester.

"Let's sit down," says Rich, pulling me onto the bed.

"I'm not ready," I say.

We neck for a while, innocently, and Rich drives me back to the dorm at three in the morning. Outside the dorm we sit for a few moments in the truck. The drifts are still and foreign. Rich leans forward, tapping the doe-skin fingers of his gloves against the steering wheel. His breath freezes on the window in peacock feathers. He's singing softly, "Hot blooded, check it and see, I got a fever of a hundred and three, I'm hot blooded, hot blooded." Then he turns to me and says, "Jill, I'm in love with you."

I swallow. "Rich, you can't be in love with me, you just met me."

He slams his fist against the dash, making me jump.

"Don't tell me how I feel, I know how I feel."

Years before this I'm a camp counsellor and a boy of twelve has a crush on me. He throws the basketball hard at my breasts and then at the velvet stage curtain in the back of the gym. He puts trouble makers in their place. "You shut up or I'll bash your face into a brick wall. You answer miss nice." One day all the kids wrestle me to the floor for a bag of chocolate kisses. This boy lands on top of me with all the other kids on top of him. Everyone is laughing, shouting. His hips grind against mine as he stretches for the Cellophane bag and suddenly he looks down at me. I'm struggling, being tickled by a thousand fingers. He screams at everyone, "Get off me, get off me." Rolling over, he lashes them with his fists. Everyone gets off and he storms out of the gym, revving his dirt bike, slapping a spray of stones at the wall of the school.

I haven't eaten anything in two days. Even orange juice hurts my mouth. I should be out there getting a job. I get up at eight and have a bath. I go upstairs to wake Mike. The bedroom is even hotter than downstairs. He says, "Lie down." When I wake up it's two o'clock. I almost miss my dentist's appointment. The assistant is blond and wears a gauze mask. She squeezes a thread of liquid from a syringe and lowers a blinding light into my eyes. She squirts some chemical into my mouth and sucks it out with a hose. Then the dentist, who has been scrubbing up to the elbow, bends for a quick glance.

"Wisdom teeth," he says with satisfaction. "You're looking at nine hundred to a thousand bucks."

"I haven't got any money."

"Then I suggest gargling with salt water." He removes his silver pick gingerly.

My mother calls later in the day. She wakes me.

"Would you please do me favour? Would you just go round to a few schools and ask them for a job? They're crying out for teachers in Toronto."

"Mom, they don't hire people who aren't qualified."

"Couldn't you pretend you didn't know that, just try?"

"Mom, don't worry, there's plenty of work up here."

"I know, but it's time you did something."

"I know."

My mother works in the office of a new insurance company. She works from eight-thirty until five as a secretary; she has two weeks off a year. Once, her boss, who is three years older than me, rang her phone and when she picked it up immediately, he said, "Good, Marsha, just wanted to make sure you got it by the first ring." My mother complained to someone in a senior position. Now she's afraid she might lose her job. At her age it would be difficult to find another. Everyone else in the office is twenty-five or twenty-six at the oldest.

Everyone has left the dorm for the long weekend. Darlene and I hitch-hike to a cabin she knows about. We heat a can of beans on the woodstove, and eat a tub of ice cream with one spoon, and then a can of Vienna sausages. Our sneakers are soaking from the rain and we put them on the woodstove to dry; the plastic soles melt, creating a stink.

We play crazy eights and talk about sex. I say, "My mother has *The Joy of Sex* hidden under her mattress. I mean she's explained the whole thing in detail, she's shown me every other how-to book published, but they got *The Joy of Sex* as a wedding present and it's like she thinks she's the only one who has a copy. Anyway, I looked at it and the drawings are in soft pencil. I mean they're really soft and gentle, even the leather and bondage section is gentle. My mother thinks that you only have sex with people you love."

We leave wearing rubber boots belonging to Darlene's brother. We hitch a ride in a pick-up. It's dark and it's not until I've slammed the door that I realize the two men have rifles on their laps. They head immediately off the highway onto a dirt road. Darlene and I say nothing, they say nothing. We bump along and I dig my fingernails into my soaking coat sleeves. They drop us at the turn-off to Stephenville. I ask Darlene, "Were you afraid?" Darlene says, "They have a moose in the back, it's out of season." As the truck pulls away I see the bulk of it in the red brake lights.

Darlene calls. Her visa has come through. I invite her to Pizza Hut. Toronto is getting the tail end of Hurricane Hugo. My feet are sloshing in my shoes. I have to wait fifteen minutes outside United Cigars watching headlights sword fighting the rain at the intersection. Then I see her. Her glasses are streaming with water. Our jeans are wet below our rain jackets while we eat our pizza, and they have the air conditioning on. Our teeth chatter while she talks about raw octopus, sleeping mats, paper walls and geisha girls. She says, "Japanese dentists are the richest men in the world, and if they're single, who knows, maybe I'll have a few teeth pulled." She's joking. We hug outside the subway and where we press together the water soaks through our chests, icy cold. Sayonara.

Mike and I have moved in with Kate and Paulo. She's a painter and he's a physics professor. They take us to their cottage up north. It's the end of summer, you can wear a sweater, but it's warm enough to swim. Kate's parents are there. They're both seventy. Her father and I swim for almost an hour. We take turns diving off a board set upon a raft. He watches me and comments, his voice strong on the silent lake, "That's a nice one, that was a lovely one." My mother was a lifeguard when she was eighteen. What I call freestyle she calls the crawl. She does the crawl with even strokes. When she teaches children to swim, she says, "If you measure your strokes you can go a long time, you can go for ever."

Kate's mother is sorting old slides. She says, "If we don't know what they are, we're throwing them out."

Kate says, "You can't do that."

"Oh, yes I can."

Kate pins a white sheet over the fireplace. We each have a hot cup of tea. I have a fever now from the infection in my teeth. There's a picture of Kate's mother and father when they had just met. They're laughing into the camera.

A picture of Kate at ten with a kitten. A jungle in Malaysia. A falling cliff face in Venezuela.

"That's the earthquake," says Kate's father. A slide of a green field covered with mist.

"Oh, I love England," says Kate's mother, and she claps her hands.

A slide of a church window. Everyone leans closer.

"Throw it out," says Kate's mother. "We don't know what it is." But her father clicks on.

"You're not throwing anything out, Dave."

A slide of a grave stone, out of focus.

Mike tucks me in bed. He rubs my body vigorously because I'm freezing cold and boiling hot.

"That's some long life together they had," I say.

I've got a job. I'm working as an assistant in an office that is publishing a directory of Canadian artists, musicians and writers. It's my job to open letters and sort the biographies alphabetically. Returned biographies with any kind of correction go in the edit pile. I call home and tell my mother I'm an assistant editor. She's relieved. I'm doing the R's. There he is. His bio is shorter than most. But he has cut a record with the Sickles. All around me, paper rustles. The real assistant editor is glued to the screen of her computer.

We agree to meet the following weekend in Corner Brook, where he has his final gig before leaving the island. He's leaving via the Port-aux-Basques ferry the next morning. This is my last chance to see him. But the highway's closed. The mall is closed and the school is closed. Everyone is stuck in the dorm. The woman who runs the snack bar downstairs is selling microwaved subs hand over fist. There's a line-up at the Pac-Man machine. Harry says he's going to Corner Brook. This is the first weekend he's allowed out of the pen. He wants a meal of home-made bread and pickled beets, a few beers with his father. Even the Heavy Equipment guys pale.

"You can't see a hand in front of you."

"You'll end up arse over kettle in a ditch."

He says I can go with him as long as I don't talk. I pack my bag. We see almost nothing for miles except abandoned cars. Harry drives with the window down so he can reach the moving windshield wipers to slap the sleet off them. Sometimes the car turns three-sixty. We go off the road and Harry makes me drive while he pushes. When he gets back inside he has icicles on his moustache. He claps me on the back with his big mitt. He says, "How well do you know this guy Rich?"

"Well, I only met him for one night, but we talked a lot."

"And you're going to stay with him, just like that?"

"He said I could have a room to myself."

"Yeah, well, why don't you stay over at mom's tonight? You could sleep with my sister."

"I'm sure I'll be okay, Harry."

In the summer evenings, once in a while, my mother mows my father's grave. She manages to get the mower in the trunk of her car by herself. His grave is near the ocean. When she finishes she lights a cigarette and sits down on the pink marble that frames the grave. She says his name out loud. I watch out the window for her to come back. Often she's back just before sunset, smelling juicy green like cut grass.

My mother phones the dorm in Stephenville. She's shaken. She says she was walking down the path to the house in the dark and she heard it before she saw it. She managed to push herself into a fir tree just in time, branches all over her face. A moose galloping up. She says she could smell it, she could

41

have touched his antler. She lost her groceries, Campbell's Soup tins tumbling into the dark.

She says the roof is leaking and she can't keep the place up by herself. My mother and father put icicles of stucco on the ceiling, it reminded them of a hotel they stayed at in Spain. Now it's falling off in clumps.

She has very set ideas about how she wants her own grave kept after she's gone.

"If I taught you anything in your whole life it's how to write a thank-you note. When I die you'll be getting lots of sympathy cards and you have to answer every one of them."

"Not on your life."

"Don't say that."

Everybody is drunk and stoned and Rich looks surprised to see me. The apartment is a lot like the one in Stephenville, wood panelling, girlie pictures, squashed cigarette butts on the tiles. Around three, everyone goes to bed. Rich leads me to the couch. I say, "Where are you going to sleep?"

"Right here with you."

"Rich, you said I could have my own bed."

He begins unbuttoning my blouse. I push his hands away. He kisses me, I kiss him back. He pulls my blouse until the first three buttons pop off. He giggles.

"I don't want to."

"I'm leaving tomorrow, baby, this is your last chance."

"I came all this way to see you."

"Well, you're going to have to come a little further."

He unzips his jeans and forces my hand down his pants, closing my fingers over his penis. He grabs my elbow and jerks my arm. He moans, "I'm going to come." I wrench my hand away.

"What are you doing?" he hisses.

"I'm sorry."

"You frigid bitch."

"I'm sorry."

"You cock tease."

"You said I could have my own room."

"Why the fuck did you come here?"

"I was lonely."

"Yeah, well, Jesus. Good night."

He rolls over, his face pressing into the couch, leaving me only the edge. This is something I can't tell my mother. This is something that would disappoint her. I open the door to the apartment, but the screen door is blocked shut. Snow has drifted to the very top of the door.

When I wake up, Rich is at the table drinking orange juice from a carton. I think of my mother's plaid chair in the morning light, the glass empty on the table beside it.

Degrees of Nakedness

The top half of Joan's house caught fire and burned while she slept downstairs. The microwave and television melted into lumps as smooth and shiny as beach rocks. She woke up to make herself a cup of tea in the morning and when she got upstairs everything was black. The furniture was in cinders. The windows were blackened with soot. She walked into the centre of the living room and looked around her. Her footsteps had exposed the green and gold shag carpet beneath the soot. It occurred to her that she must be asleep.

She went back downstairs and sat on the edge of her bed. Then she went upstairs again. She picked up the phone but it was dead. Her greenish gold footsteps were the only colour in the room. It reminded her of Dorothy on her way to the Emerald City.

The fire chief said it was a miracle Joan was still alive. The temperature had risen to three thousand degrees. There were

large double-paned patio windows. The inside panes had broken but the fire ran out of oxygen before the outside panes
could break. The fire chief said if the second pane had broken
or if she had gotten up in the middle of the night and opened
the back door, the house would have exploded. Joan said she
felt as if she had been stripped.

She and her twelve-year-old son, Wiley, moved in with us.
Wiley had been at his grandmother's the night of the fire. Joan
says she keeps having the same nightmare. Her hand on the
doorknob of the back door. Everything in sharp focus, like
before a storm. Wiley is standing outside the door, in the forest.
In the dream, Wiley is a baby. Joan knows she can't open the
door; he's toddling through the woods to the highway. He
waves to her the way he first learned to wave, with both hands,
the fingers pointed toward himself. Her palm is sweaty, and she
turns the knob. The house blows up. In the dream, she sees
two-by-fours twirling into the sky like batons.

One night, during the dream, she reaches for the glass of
water by the bed and throws it over herself. She wakes because
she smacked the bridge of her nose with the glass, and water is
running down her nightdress, between her breasts, down her
belly. She has a little half-moon bruise on the bridge of
her nose.

I have become interested in nakedness. All the different kinds.
Especially since my sister-in-law moved in. It's as if she can't
keep herself covered. Things always seem to slip away from her.
I walked in on her in the bath once. Her skin was tanned in the

shape of her bathing suit. The skin of her torso seemed very white, the colour of a tree when you strip off the bark.

I have this idea for an art exhibit. I want to get myself photographed all over town, nude. Sitting on a bench in Bannerman Park, reading the newspaper, riding my bike past the Salvation Army and Bowring's, sitting on the War Memorial with a take-out coffee. I'll keep a wrap-around dress nearby in case anybody shows up. I figure it can be done at five in the morning when nobody's around.

Before supper, my husband, Mike, shoves Joan out the front door and locks it. There's a small square window in the front door. Joan has her face pressed against it. She's giggling, and saying, "Come on now Mike, let me in."

There are seven neighbourhood boys armed with water balloons standing in a semi-circle around her, arms raised.

Mike puts his face to the window so he can meet Joan's eyes and quietly lifts the mail slot, sticks a pistol through and squirts, hitting the crotch of her jeans. It takes her a moment to realize what's happening. Then Wiley, who has gone to the third floor, opens the window over the front door and drops a wobbling balloon on her head. She shrieks. The boys open fire, and balloons splat against her. The breeze changes direction. At the end of the street eight girls are lined up from one sidewalk to the other. They seem to be advancing to the music of the sea cadets' band in the Star of the Sea Hall at the end of the street. Each one has a swollen balloon, held like a baby. The boys are still for a second, then one of them yells, "Run!"

and they tear down the street, their sneakers slapping on the pavement. Mike lets Joan inside.

I've persuaded Joan to go to the only strip joint in town with me the next night. I just want to see what it's like. A woman can't get in without a male escort. Joan's hair is very short, and she's going to dress like a man to get us in. The newspaper ad says formal wear required. The woman on the phone said that means no construction boots or torn shirts. I dig out the tuxedo Mike wore to our wedding for Joan to wear.

I'm not usually one for telling strangers things but I've gotten into the habit of telling the woman who sells the coffee and muffins in the cafeteria of the building where I work the most intimate things about myself. Early in the morning, the ugly cafeteria is huge and empty; my footsteps echo as in a cathedral. Usually, it's just the two of us at that hour. She wears a brown polyester suit with two seams down the front, and a gold bull horn on a chain around her neck. Sometimes when I fall asleep I can see that horn and the skin of her neck. The exact location of her mole, the tiny gold horn jiggling while she wipes the counter. When I give her a twenty she looks at me as if I should know better. She says with her eyebrow arched, "Are you trying to break me?"

Sometimes, just as I'm dropping off to sleep, I see her arched eyebrow, exaggerated, and a disconnected voice "Are you trying to break me?"

I have told her, for instance, that my sister-in-law has moved in because her house burned down, that Joan hates her ex-husband, and that we have no idea when she will move out. That my husband had a daughter with another woman, before he met me. Sometimes we have the child over for supper. I have told the cafeteria woman I believe Joan got drunk and set fire to the house on purpose. Often I find myself saying to her, "Strange old world, isn't it?" and shaking my head like an old man. She wears a plastic name tag that says "Cathy." Once I said, "Good morning, Cathy," and she said, "That's not my real name."

At the dinner table, Mike says, "Joan, I bought you a little present."

Mike drops a tape into the tape deck. It's Herb Alpert and the Tijuana Brass. Joan squeals with delight and jumps up to dance to "Tijuana Taxi." At the end of all the big brass, there's a deep honking sound. Joan wiggles and struts, and when the honk comes, she sticks her bum out. Then she falls onto the floor, giggling. From the floor, she wheezes, "That's what Mike and I did when we were kids."

Wiley takes this opportunity to scrape his broccoli into the garbage. I take a single triangle of cold pizza out of the fridge, hold the pizza in front of my crotch, lay a bunch of bananas on my head, and start miming a striptease while the Tijuana Brass do their thing. Joan drags herself off the floor, pulling herself up by the rungs in the chair, still panting with laughter, and starts to drink her coffee. We tell Wiley, "Okay, okay, settle down." But when another honk comes, Joan almost chokes and the coffee comes out of her nose. She is snorting and choking, her eyes watering. Wiley says, "Jeez, Mom, will you give it up?"

With the fourth honk, Joan bursts into tears. Mike turns off the tape. "For God's sake, Joan." I point my fork and a limp piece of broccoli at Mike. "Leave her alone, she's allowed to cry." Joan has been bursting into tears a lot since the fire.

Joan's last boyfriend broke up with her two or three nights before the fire. She says he was a real sweetie. She slapped a newspaper at his chest outside a restaurant and it bounced off and fell between a mail box and a newspaper vending box. It's still there. We walk past it on the way to the supermarket. It's waterlogged and you can see she twisted it in her fists before she flung it at him.

I remember the cover of the album, Herb Alpert and the Tijuana Brass. A naked woman covered in whipped cream, the heart-shaped swirls of cream covering her breasts, she licking a blob of cream from a long red fingernail. One smooth long leg parts the soft folds of cream, almost up to her hip. You can almost taste that cream in the brass music.

Later that night, when Wiley is in bed, Mike and I fight. I throw my cup of coffee across the room as hard as I can. The cup hits the wall behind his head and leaves a mark in the gyprock like a frown. There are no curtains on the front window. It's dark outside and the living room is lit like a fish tank. A woman in a cotton skirt with a black palm leaf print is standing on the opposite sidewalk under a street lamp, arms crossed over her breasts. She is watching our fight as if it were a movie. Then, on our side of the street, two heads pass under the window, a man and a woman. They wave, surprised to see us. Mike's face is stiff with anger, but both of us wave back, uncertainly. They knock on the door. It turns out they were neighbours of ours two years ago. We hardly spoke to them then and haven't seen them since, but they seem delighted to see us. Mike and I stand in the doorway to talk to them. I can feel the snarl on my face thaw. The breeze is warm and it rushes through the trees on the traffic island as if it can't make up its mind which way to go.

The guy is tanned and carrying a tennis racket. He mimes taking swings as he talks. He says, "Yeah, I was away studying giant clams, they weigh as much as fifty kilos. The shells don't really shut all the way, you can stick your whole arm in there, it's real fleshy. Isn't it, honey?" he says to his girlfriend. "They'll suck your whole arm for hours if you let 'em. The islanders say that clam flesh is an aphrodisiac, makes the adolescent penis grow or something. You know, they're a small people down there, aren't they, honey? They used to joke about how big I was, they said Barb must be a happy woman."

Barb smiles up at him. Her mouth glitters, unexpectedly, with braces. "Oh, they thought Tony was real big."

When Mike shuts the door, he says, "That cup could have killed me."

I say, "Are you trying to break me?"

Then he gets a cloth from the kitchen and wipes the splattered coffee off the wall. Joan walks in at that moment, sees the broken cup and leaves.

When Mike and I make love, a blush comes into his cheeks and the tips of his ears. That's my private colour for him, almost plum. The first time we were together we were behind the row housing under criss-crossing clotheslines, white shirts laughing with their bellies. We were drunk and his tongue in my ear sounded like a pot of mussels boiling, the shells opening, the salty shells clicking off one another, a riot of tiny noises. I got the flu. He made a pot of tea: cinnamon, cloves, apple and orange chunks. The next day we made love in his new house, empty of furniture except for a couch, covered with satiny parakeets, belonging to the former owners. Streetlight poured in. A plastic bag of chicken breasts glowed on the floor where I'd dropped it. I had been swimming in a hotel pool that day where they sold paper bathing suits. I made Mike close his eyes, and I put on the damp suit, which smelled of chlorine and was indestructible.

Once Mike did a tour of a glass blowing factory. They chose him out of the tour group to do the blowing. When we first met he gave me an irregular perfume bottle with his breath caught in the bubbles. I've worn lilac since I was thirteen. When he took the stopper off, it surprised me that it smelled like myself. Lilac on the sanded wand he rubbed down my neck, sticky and warm. It was as if he had trapped all my years in a bottle, then tickled them down my neck. Now he wants to leave for a year, to work. I don't want him to go. I need him here. I'm afraid of him leaving. It looks as though Joan and I will share an apartment if he leaves.

Today, around five, the doorbell buzzes and it's Jill, a little girl who plays with Wiley. The street is full of squad cars. The police are putting on bullet proof vests. They take rifles and guns out of the trunks of the cars and load them with bullets. A cop comes to the door. Pushing Jill from behind, he says, "Can she stay in there? She can't go around the corner."

I ask what's going on, my voice shrill. The cop looks as if he's going to answer me but then he turns away and trots down the street with the gun. A CBC van arrives. Some guy coming up the street says there's a man in one of the houses around the corner with a gun. Princess Anne had been on George Street earlier in the day. I'd taken Wiley and a bunch of neighbourhood kids to see her. It must be a sniper who has run up from George Street. Wiley is on the concrete step of the house across the street, eating a supper of Jiggs dinner a neighbour has given him. The cop cars glitter between us and I say, "Get over here."

"What about my supper?"

"Just get over here." He comes over with the plate. I phone Jill's mother, Maureen, to tell her Jill is with us. A cop answers the phone.

"Sergeant Peddle," she says.

I say, "Can I talk to Maureen?"

She says, "I wish you could, but I can't get her down. What do you want?"

I say I just wanted to tell her her daughter's at my house, I'm a neighbour.

"The daughter's at your house." Sergeant Peddle hangs up.

I whisper to Mike, "The man with the gun is in Maureen's house."

We met Maureen through Wiley. Maureen's a lesbian. We've never seen much of her partner, who's a surgeon. They keep pretty much to themselves, but since Joan moved in, she and Maureen have called each other every now and then to ask if the other would mind babysitting for half an hour.

After twenty minutes the cops pull away, but the CBC is still there with the cameras. Jill wants to go home. I phone Maureen. The phone rings for some time before she picks it up. I hear long sobs. I keep saying, "Maureen?" but she just sobs into the phone, no words. I tell her I'm Joan's sister-in-law, and I say, "I have your daughter here." She doesn't say anything. I say, "Do you want me to come down?"

"Yes."

The large glass window in the front door of Maureen's house is smashed in. Broken glass covers the concrete steps. Inside, the plush carpet crunches with every step. I call out to her. In the hall, two framed paintings have been torn off the wall, the frames cracked in half. Maureen is in the kitchen with her head in her arms on the table. The window beside her is smashed. The contents of the fridge lie all over the floor, and the glass shelves have been torn out of it. Some kind of orange drink has been spilled on the floor, so as I walk across to the table my sneakers make a sound like ripping cotton. I put my arms around Maureen and put one hand over hers. I rub the back of her thumb with mine. I say, "Who was it? Who did this? Was there a man with a gun in here?" She shakes her head. "Was it your ex-husband?" She shakes her head.

I let go of her and turn on the kettle. I realize I don't know her at all. There are three giant yellow tubs of margarine lying on their sides. It seems like an incredible amount of margarine.

I can't believe how much damage there is. I think about the kind of rage it would take to sustain this much damage. I think about the damage the fire caused in Joan's house. I feel very tired. It seems utterly still. I say, "Where's your partner? Can I call her for you? Does your partner know this has happened?" The phone book is open beside Maureen. "Let me call your partner for you."

Maureen raises her head. Her eyes are sunken and blood-shot from crying or alcohol. "This was my partner," she says.

I sit down.

"This was your partner," I repeat. "She did this. How did the cops get here?" I am afraid. The kettle whistles. "Where are the tea bags?" She points.

"She's caused over twenty-five hundred dollars' worth of damage in the last three months. I've had to replace every window more than once. She won't let me out. She won't let me see anyone. She'll be back, she'll kill me tonight, I can't get away from her. If she was a man I would have done something, I wouldn't have put up with it. But it's taken my mother so long to understand. How could I tell them?"

The breeze blows gently through the window. It is the sunniest day we've had in a long time. You can hear some of the music from the Canada Day celebrations. I ask about the cops.

"I was sitting on the front step and the glass showered down on top of me and I said by Jesus that's the last time she'll break a window in my house. When Tom, my neighbour, came through the door, I was in the process, I was proceeding to kill her. I said, Tom, call the cops, please. They came in and arrested her."

Somebody knocks on the door. Maureen crumples.

"Please don't let anyone in."

I walk out over the glass. A man is standing outside. He says, "I'm with the CBC. Can you tell us what happened here? We heard someone was arrested."

I say, "Well, it's pretty insensitive to come around here right now, isn't it?"

He says, "We don't know what happened, that's all."

I say, "Nobody here's going to tell you." It strikes me how absurd it is to speak to him through the broken window without opening the door. Down the street, a man is pointing a camera at us.

Then Maureen and I drink the tea. We sit in silence until the phone rings. It's Mike. He asks if everything is okay. He says he is going to order the kids a pizza. I say that sounds good. I tell Maureen Jill can sleep at our house. We get a broom and start to clean up. Maureen hauls out a big sheet of plastic she has for sealing broken windows.

When I get home, Joan is dressed in Mike's tuxedo. She hasn't heard anything about the incident on the street and is dressed to go to the strip joint. I expect the dancers to be ugly in some way, but they have beautiful bodies. They dance on a raised stage and the bottom of it is covered with mirror. I have never been in this bar before. They have ultra-violet lighting that seems to erase everything in the room except whiteness. The women wear white G-strings so their crotches glow as if they are floating. There's a man in a dark suit and tie sitting at the table in front of me. I glance up and see him in the mirrors around the bottom of the stage. The mirrors reflect him from the neck down; his head is above stage level. His white collar is glowing, sharply cut. At first glance, it looks like a headless body. I watch his hand in the mirror, lifting his Scotch and aiming it at the empty neck of his shirt.

Joan and I are loaded, walking home past the Anglican cathedral. She starts to cry. I never hug people. I'm not a very physical person. But I hug her suddenly. I draw her body into mine and I grab her hair in my fingers. It shocks me when I realize I have a fistful of her hair in my hand and it is the exact texture of my husband's. She's wearing one of my husband's jackets over the tuxedo. The jacket is gold silk. It looks like a wedding band on him. It has started to rain on our way home, while Joan is crying. The rain falls in giant splotches on the quilted jacket, making it heavy and tarnished.

Meet Me in Sidi Ifni

Look for me in Sidi Ifni. I'm leaving the back yard. Those weeds you spent half the summer thrashing have returned unscarred, thicker, greener, and the perfume from them makes the air moist. They grew back when you stopped to have a bottle of pop. We can't just stop like that.

These are the things I'm leaving. I'm leaving the toys all over the stairs. That magic wand with the glow-in-the-dark star sitting on the coffee table, so that if you walk into the living room at night it seems to float. The paperweight with the unicorn and the snowstorm you shake. It's May and we haven't taken down the Christmas wreath from the back door, but the stuffed dove is under the kitchen table on its back, beak open, claws stretched forward. I'm leaving my water colours in the cookie tin.

Once we made love in a blackout. There were brass candle holders in sluffing drifts of wax. At the bottom of Cathedral

Street cars swished their tails like lethargic crocodiles. Engines straining.

You said, I'll blow out the candles.

The wicks curled to protect themselves, flared orange against your breath, then out.

You said, Over here on the chair.

A passing headlight gleamed on the worn rose brocade of the armchair, and where the covering is torn, the stuffing and a coiled spring, just by the inside of your wrist. The shadows of the rubber plants climbed across the ceiling like blind crustaceans, and crawled back into themselves when the car passed.

People will see, I said.

But the whole island is dark.

Saliva soaked, water colours bled from your fingers. Burnt sienna spine, cherries on my nipples, ink black strokes. My knees dug into the back corners of the chair around your waist. I rose and dropped over the wavelets of frost on the window like a mermaid. A horn honked. And honked and honked.

Never mind, you whispered, never mind.

I'm leaving the cockroaches in the shower on the dirty tiles and all the foreign coins we saved for parking meters.

Your daughter, who doesn't know how to swim, almost choking me, terror-locks her arms around my neck. Her naked body shivers, lips bluish, she squeals in a shrill pitch. Then we look into each other's eyes, our noses almost touching. I'm trying to make her remember me always. She opens her mouth suddenly and shrieks and bashes her fist in the water. Her magnetic letters on the fridge arrange themselves, HA HA HA.

I'm leaving on the train. The first train we rode together. Holding each other on the narrow cot, people on both the cots beneath us. The darkness squeezing down on the train so it vibrated, the vibration passing through us into our toes. The conductor shook his black ringlets when he ripped the morning sunshine through the curtain.

Sunlight falling through the slatted roof over the souks, striping the brass pots, diagonals over your face, your freckled arms. The snake charmer tipping the lid off the woven basket with his big toe. Earthy coloured pyramids of spice, a boy with a bright green lizard on his outstretched palm. Don't forget the German toy maker who could find his way by facing the sun. His spectacles pressed into his flushed cheeks like teeth biting apples. The sturdy way he set down his feet, two puffs of dust. Dripping loops of dyed fabric, fuchsia, turquoise, the odour of urine, light piercing the loose weave.

I'm going to Sidi Ifni. I'm leaving the shadows from the venetian blinds on the kitchen table and the fridge that makes so much noise it sounds like a spaceship. I can't wait all night for you to move. You survey the board with your eyes squinted up, your beer bottle cuddled near your crotch, and then with a gesture of triumph you shoot a bishop across the board and put your own king in check.

Look for me in Sidi Ifni. The Spanish conquered it. An old man pushes a wheelbarrow filled with sizzling donuts glazed and hissing like wasps. Remember him? The ocean barely lifts its lip. It behaves like a pond. I'll hire the blue Mercedes with the miniature weather vane on the hood. The windshield is cracked, and inside the car smells like American cigarettes.

I'll leave from Tiznit, silver capital of the country. There's a salesman there who claims he is the grandson of the chief of the caravan. He wears an Adidas jacket under his djellaba and accepts credit cards. I'll leave in the middle of a festival, when the streets are squeezed full of people, shoulder to shoulder. Boys in tree branches, boiled eggs, mandarins in dusty plastic bags. Women with tambourines, singing from their throats, heads thrown back. They hold in the air gowns on crucifixes with bushes of mint stuffed in the necks. The dignitaries drive their cars over Persian carpets and are showered with rose petals.

What was that woman's name? The Swedish woman in the tight floral print. She was a chaise longue, soft as a swimming pool. You think I didn't smell her kitchen, all crushed camomile and coconut suntan oil? Oh, you could sleep in with her, the phone company would come and disconnect the alarm clock by mistake. Her seeds sprout as she flings them. She made me mince my garlic. I said she was dewy-eyed, bucolic. But you would remind me, her caesar salad's creamy and her pubic hair is magenta. I'll be in Sidi Ifni.

The taxi driver's horn will blast, nasal singing, fast impossible banjo. We'll drive as fast as that.

I'll be running a hotel of pink chalky colour. The paint is peeling in the shape of continents and oceans that I can read like tea leaves.

I'll have an affair with the projectionist from the movie theatre. The theatre has many smashed light bulbs in its sign. He speaks only Spanish and grunts "*Me gusta*" while he grinds. The film in the noisy projector. You on the screen. You on the highway where the car broke down, in your yellow rain coat. You, swallowed by the fog of Signal Hill. You, jerking your body to screaming Bob Dylan in the kitchen. Your voice through the wall, overanimated, reading your daughter bedtime stories. You, crouched with the hose waiting for your sister, spraying your mother by mistake, spraying all the years away from her, so when she scurried back inside, her face looked like she was fourteen.

I'll be dancing with my Spanish ghost in the dust. We'll dance the tango, very seriously. Sweat makes my make-up run, and our cheeks are pressed together. We'll smell of gin that has come through our skin in the thinnest film. His coarse moustache will tickle. He'll say, "*Me amore, Me amore*" — and then you — having ridden on Air Canada, a rickety bus and finally a blue Mercedes — you will burst through the doors, crushing the rusty locks in your fist. You will be wearing your jeans and suspenders, but instead of that pink T-shirt, you will for once have dressed for the occasion, a white cotton shirt with pirate sleeves. You will pull out a sword. One by one you will pop the buttons off the shirt of my Spanish troubadour. They will fall to the floor with a click click that resembles the grinding of your teeth.

Carmen Has Gonorrhoea

I'm wishing for Carmen to get hit by a cement truck. I've thrown pennies in the mall fountain wishing for that. Muttering with my eyes closed. Cement truck, cement truck, cement truck. A crisp winter night, a hint of wood smoke in the air, stars like little pieces of glass, and the cement truck, snorting exhaust, waiting on top of Barter's Hill. Lots of vehicles lose their brakes on Barter's Hill. Twice in the past three years cars have careened down the hill and smashed through Lar's Fruit Store. I lie on my bed and wish for that cement truck so hard I get cross-eyed. There's a crack in the plaster on my bedroom ceiling, coming out from the light fixture. I stare at that crack until it starts to move like a hand on a clock, around and around. Carmen's days are numbered, like a radar scan swooping, swooping. Where are you, Carmen?

She's at Bar Baric. It's Fetish Night. There's a children's plastic swimming pool in the corner filled with chocolate pudding.

Two men will wrestle in white boxer shorts printed with little hearts. Later, two waitresses will clean the men's bodies. On Fetish Night the barmaids wear yellowish lettuce leaves over their breasts, dangle green grapes from their nipples and spank willing customers with palm leaves.

Carmen sings Bossa Nova. She says she had to leave Eddie to pursue her rising star. She wears a Spanish dress made of embossed leather and a black feather boa that she weasels over the paunches in the front row. You can bet Eddie is among the paunches. Some say Carmen's power lies in the castanets. She takes a big breath and raises her arms over her head. You'd think she was going to dive off the cliffs in Acapulco while the tide was out. Then she starts. She gives them one snap and every neck in the bar twists like a wrung chicken. Those castanets are second nature to Carmen, claws on a crab. Her mother swears she could hear Carmen snapping her fingers while she was still in the womb. The first few snaps are like the hooves of bulls pawing the Formica tabletops. Then complicated rhythms squirm and writhe over each other. Carmen has the whole bar filled with black bulls in heat. Every one of those slack-jowled husbands searches for himself in the smoky, gold-flecked mirror behind her. He's searching for his own pasty face, but what he finds looking back is a matador.

I never would have resorted to the cement trucks if other plans hadn't failed. One night I was down at Bar Baric with a tube of crazy glue. Carmen had her back turned and in a couple of seconds, that's all it took, I had the castanets glued together, like a couple of clam shells. She got up there, raised her arms over her head, looked down the end of her nose, and there wasn't a click out of her. I thought I had her. But that was the night she started playing the spoons. When she finishes her number she does this spontaneous dive from the stage. The crowd on the dance floor catches her in its arms and lifts her overhead.

Every night they chant, "Carmen, Carmen, Carmen." I can hear them from my bed. Her name thunders up the hills of downtown, raises the hairs on the leaves of geraniums in the windows of Gower Street, makes the light turn green at Rawlins Cross, grows softer, ticklish, near our split-level behind the Avalon Mall. But you can hear them chanting her name, even up here you can hear it, just barely, like a feather on your skin when you're sleeping. I can see Eddie's pink ear straining for it, straining, straining. It makes the curtain ripple against the hardwood floor as if a cat was stretching against it. I dig my fingernails into Eddie's back. Peek-a-boo, Carmen. Come out, come out, wherever you are!

Eddie drops off. I can't sleep. I'm feverish. I throw off the sheets and rip open the sheers of our bedroom window. The lawns of all the houses between my house and the mall spread out before me. New frost stiffens them. Beyond is the mall parking lot. Blood rushes to my cheeks. Five gleaming cement trucks are parked there, hulking and silent under the street-lights.

When I go to work in the morning, the red and white bellies of the trucks are already grinding hungrily, flopping over the cement inside. Their white cabs gleam like teeth. I feel delicious shivers. I work the cash at Woolco. Mornings, the machine hums under my fingers. The register imitates that grinding, the hunger of the machine that will bring Carmen down, flatten her. The manager pats my polyester pant leg.

"You're looking animated, we sure like that," he says.

I imagine the actual impact, the thud, the ka-thunk of the front wheels, the ka-thunk of the back. Then, from the tail, spewing thick blobs of cement on her squashed carcass until she's a slab of grey stone. If I could be there when it happened I'd tie a rope onto her remains, maybe onto her bony hand with that hypocritical little ring with the peace symbol sticking out the top. The fingers crooked as if grasping a last handful of breath. I'd haul her to the harbour. Dump. Let all the sewers of the city spill over her. Ha.

Lots of women hate Carmen, so I'm not alone. But lots of women forgive her, fall out of rank in the army of hatred. Which is disappointing.

Eddie's mother, for example, likes Carmen a lot better than she likes me. Oh, she's had the wool pulled, let me tell you. Gert sells life insurance and not much gets past her. We'll all be sitting down to Christmas dinner and she'll bring up Carmen. "How's Carmen, Eddie?" The syrup in her voice.

Or on St. Patrick's Day: "Carmen's a lovely woman, isn't she, Merle?" I tried to show a little creativity with the potato salad, a little green food colouring, and for dessert, little jelly shamrocks. Does anybody mention those special touches? No, it's all Carmen, Carmen, Carmen. Merle is Eddie's dad. Merle had a real thing for Carmen, even while she was his daughter-in-law. That's the kind of family I've married into. Gert had no problem turning a blind eye to that, but she's down at my house running her finger over the dust on the windowsill every other afternoon, turning up her nose at the socks on the stairs, the garbage piled up in the laundry room. The diapers in the toilet. "Do you hear much from Carmen?" ask his sisters, "I guess she's pretty busy now that she's cutting those records?"

They'd all like to see me fail. Eddie's sisters work on the grill in the Woolco cafe. They'd do anything to have my position, head cash. The jealousy makes them spiteful. I can't blame them, working under those heat lamps all day with the grease from the deep fryers. There's nothing less attractive than a hairnet under a paper hat, and neither of them are married. As far as they're concerned there isn't another man as wonderful as the baby, Eddie, and there's nobody good enough for him, either. Except, of course, Carmen.

Carmen and Eddie still have long conversations on the phone. She's into the whole Goddess thing, and she wants to share that. She's always talking witch burnings, prisms, tidal pulls, tea leaves, crystal balls. She's got no money to pay the heating bill, but she's got a bigger crystal ball on layaway. The crystal ball she has is too small for her purposes. I mean we all have to pay the heating bill, right?

"Yeah, I got a bigger crystal ball on layaway," she smiles to Eddie, her chin in the palm of her hand, the candlelight flickering over her cheekbones.

"Who in the name of Christ puts crystal balls on layaway?" I scream at Eddie, after she leaves.

I mean, why bigger? Why a bigger crystal ball? Is there a better picture or something? Have they got a warehouse full of crystal balls on an empty prairie somewhere out west that pulses with unnatural light every equinox?

How does she pay for them? Nobody makes any money singing Bossa Nova, I don't care how far her voice carries. I'll tell you how Carmen makes her money. Admirers. She must have had every disease on the go, believe me. Who do you think went down to that alley outside the Bar Baric and spray-painted "Carmen has Gonorrhoea"? Fluorescent orange. Ha. Most of the wives in town banned her from the spiritual healing retreat. They had a vote. How could they do otherwise? Half the women there were trying to heal a wound Carmen caused. Women baring the lacerations of their hearts, moaning at the loss of their breadwinners, their brothers, their fathers. Carmen has caused more than half of the spiritual carnage downtown.

But no more. The cement trucks are charged. I can feel their power vibrating like jackhammers through my body. I walked home from the mall today, too exhilarated for public transport. I entered every street on the way home just in time to see a cement truck pulling around the distant corner. There must be a convoy a hundred strong. In the kitchen Eddie can't understand why I'm in such a good mood. I chuck him under the chin. "Cha-cha-cha," I say to him, enigmatically. Soon he will be asleep in front of the football game.

I'm standing on Barter's Hill. Carmen is just leaving the bar. We see her pass, beneath one streetlight after another. Then, there she is, outlined in the flashing lights of Lar's Fruit Store. Carmen is silhouetted against a pyramid of delicately balanced bananas reaching from floor to ceiling. I have her where I want her. I let the red flag rip through the air and savour the cutting whisper it makes. This is for you, Eddie. This is for our marriage. The headlights of one hundred cement trucks come on at once. Carmen is stunned in the brilliant glare, her body pressed against the glass window. There is the deafening noise of one hundred cement truck engines. Even if she could reach for her castanets, nobody would hear anything over that noise. They are charging, charging cement trucks.

Then another noise, unearthly, like lobsters dropped in boiling water, amplified a thousandfold. I cover my ears with my fists. The sound of one hundred cement trucks screeching their brakes. It is the sound of those same cement trucks stopping inches away from Carmen's long legs. After a moment, the trucks roll over. They lie on their backs at Carmen's feet, like playful puppies.

Surge

Giselle is supposed to go with her mother for a picnic. She's left messages on her mother's answering machine, but her mother is working toward a deadline, and not answering the phone. We're in the back seat of the car, at the Quik Stop parking lot. There's no breeze. The picnic was supposed to be at two. It's almost four. Giselle's arm is damp against mine, the moistness of a pound cake. She is wearing a pair of taupe shorts belonging to me, stained with blood or raspberries, and a shirt of mine. The armhole of the shirt hangs too low and I can see her breast, white newness, barely a breast at all. She notices my glance and tucks the material under her arm. She has a fitting tonight for shoes and a dress for her uncle's wedding.

Giselle laughs for no reason, tilting her head back.

I say, If that candy touches my shirt.

Her eyes are brilliant, the darkest blue with splinters of a lighter blue. I find it dizzying to try and understand her by looking into her eyes. Neither of her parents wears glasses and the colour of Giselle's eyes seems to suggest she's inherited sharp vision. I saw Giselle and her mom at a distance last weekend, at the park. Giselle held her body with a particular kind of grace, exactly like her mother's. Anyone could tell they were mother and daughter without even seeing their faces.

She's with us for two weeks, then she's with her mother. Everything changes in two weeks. Her clothes. A different shirt. Sometimes I realize she's taller. Her face changes so fast. I'm trying to keep up with her. She glances out the window. Something has caught her attention.

My mother is phoning right now, she says. I can hear it.

For a second I think Giselle is hearing a ring from one of the houses down the street. Then I understand she means the phone is echoing through our empty house several blocks away.

I can tell, she says. Whenever she's calling, I can tell.

Her moist face, new freckles, so close to me on the hot upholstery of the back seat. She and her mother love each other with something as hard and strong as metal scraping metal, something that can produce sparks. She's sucking a sticky piece of candy, translucent red, the wrapper crushed around the bottom, candied saliva in the creases of the Cellophane. A glassy bead of spit hangs in a thread of her hair. Her lips are neon. She has artificial strawberry breath.

There are five of us. My step-daughter, Giselle, my son, Owen, my husband, Wayne, and our daughter, Jill, who has just turned four. When we got married Wayne squeezed my fingers so tightly it hurt. He held my hand against his breastbone so that my arm was raised, as if I wanted to ask a question. Owen was rigid in a fuchsia cummerbund and pleated shirt. He was in the grip of a fever but no one noticed until later. His cheeks flaming, eyes bright. He held a tiny satin pillow for the rings. He was eight. Last Saturday night, just before dawn, I saw him in the kitchen and he was so tall I thought he was a stranger who had wandered in from the street. He was buttering a piece of bread.

Giselle wore a wine velvet dress with a satin rosebud pocket which fits Jill now.

Once Wayne happened on Owen and Giselle roughhousing on Giselle's bed, under the blankets. Wayne called me into the bathroom, shut the door. We turned to the mirror and watched each other while we tried to talk. Was it just innocent tickling? Mentioning it would make them so self-conscious. Wayne picked up his toothbrush and brushed his teeth. I watched him. There was a knock. Giselle and Owen were standing in the hall. Wayne and I came out of the bathroom. We were all embarrassed, standing near the banister. Giselle said, What's happened?

Owen is lifting a small pizza out of the oven with an egg turner. Heat radiating from the oven in the warm room. The kitchen is lit by the lamp over the fridge. There's a boy sitting at the table, his head down, wearing a baseball cap. It's after midnight, I'm just getting home.

Can Tommy sleep over? Owen says.

Tommy's hair is reddish gold, light from the lamp falling on his bent neck.

The overhead light doesn't work and at night the kitchen is dark except the small lamp on top of the fridge. The leaves of a bush move against the kitchen window and there's enough light in one patch to show the greenness, the edges of the leaves. The rest of the glass reflects the kitchen.

Owen slides the pizza on the plate between Tommy's wrists. The boy looks at my reflection in the window. His eyes are large. Owen is grim. His cheeks flushed from the stove. He says to me, Come here.

We step outside the kitchen and Owen closes the door.

He looks at the floor and says, His parents kicked him out.

Owen's breath smells of beer.

Then he opens the door and we go back into the kitchen. Giselle wanders in from the den. She bends over a Tupperware bowl of Jell-O sitting on the counter. She stares deeply at her reflection in the ruby surface, then jerks the bowl; her face wobbles like flame.

Owen says, Get your hair out of it.

She knows something is strange, and leaves the room without fight or comment.

Do your parents know where you are, Tommy? I say.

He doesn't look up from the pizza. He speaks quietly.

They don't care.

Would you mind if I called them, Tommy, just to say that you're safe?

No, I wouldn't mind.

He gives me the phone number and I sit on the stairs in the hall so he can hear what I say. It's quarter to one.

The father answers.

I say, Mr. Canning? I'm calling about Tommy.

I'll pass you over to Mary, he says.

I say my name and that Tommy is here, he'd like to sleep over if that's okay with you.

She says, Did you know Tommy's not staying at home?

No, I didn't.

He's not staying at home but I've known where he is through the grapevine every night since he's been gone. Parents have called. We'd like him to come home. But he can't seem to live by the house rules.

Well, he's here tonight, I thought I'd let you know.

I know Owen, she says. He's safe with Owen.

Good night then, I say.

Yes, she says, good night.

I think about that man saying, I'll pass you over to Mary. They're a rich family. A large front lawn, and back. Mature trees. A swimming pool, Owen says.

The smell of pizza filling the kitchen. The reddish blond hair on his bent neck in the small light. His arms resting on either side of the plate. Then picking up the knife and fork as if they were heavy.

His mother had sounded like she had just remembered why he wasn't home. The house rules. Some reason a stranger on the phone might grasp. Both of them awake at quarter to one. But the man isn't anxious enough to say for himself, Where is he now? Is he safe? I can feel his impotence through the phone, like a surge then loss of electrical power, the house brighter, as if the light were breathed in and exhaled, no light at all. The kettle stops bubbling, voices drain from the radio, the humming of things we can't hear until they've stopped. He passed me to his wife so fast I know they were lying side by side.

Giselle comes in the front door. When the front door opens it creates a vacuum in the hall and the back door slams, making us all jump. The shoes. I can see them from the kitchen. She is standing in the hall, her feet together, looking down at them. I come out and look, leaning my shoulder against the wall. A clean cream with a decorative swirl of gold metal, a small heel. They are shoes for a grown-up girl. Slippery-soled.

Wayne asks, What's happening with that boy, Tommy?

He's sleeping here again.

What are we going to do?

I don't know.

We have to do something.

Owen says Tommy slept until late in the afternoon. Came down for a bowl of cereal, his face flaming. Owen says he's embarrassed.

I tell Giselle to take some books to her room. She says, No. Anger rising with the delicate precision of a cardhouse. Our voices, curiously, getting weaker. I see it in her face, that I can't make her. For the first time. Her face blooms with it, like fireworks. Her eyes. She's excited, exhilarated. I am genuinely shocked to see that she hates me. For a split second, a spark of hate. I'm awed.

Last year we lived in Toronto for six months. Giselle stayed here with her mother. I wrote Giselle a letter every day. One night I got out of bed in my nightdress to mail it. The box was a few doors down and I ran to it in my bare feet.

We flew her up for Thanksgiving weekend. She sobbed at the zoo. We'd seen too much, walked too far. The lethargic baboon, slump-shouldered, defeated, bending to show the audience his brilliant anus. I carried Jill on my shoulders. Giselle sat on the curb while we waited for the bus to go home, rubbing her wet face on the rough sleeve of Wayne's jacket. Geese roamed near her, honking a sympathetic undertow beneath her sobs. The heavy sky threatened rain. I lifted Jill from my shoulders and for a moment I felt as if I were floating. She crouched beside Giselle and watched her cry with wonder. In the subway I said, Let's see if we can hold our breath until the next stop. Giselle said, I was thinking the exact same thing.

Jill had a necklace with a tiny bottle and bubble wand attached. She waved the wand. Bubbles. They floated in the stagnant air as if we were under water. Giselle and I gasped for breath.

I know she won't bring the books to her room so I snatch them out of her hand.

Get out of my way.

What? she says.

Her exhilaration is gone now. She's scared.

I take the stairs two at a time.

She says, I was going to.

Shut up, Giselle.

I've never said shut up to her before. Five minutes later, in the kitchen, she has forgotten. She's talking about a gypsy costume.

When we get back from the Quik Stop, Giselle's mother has left a message on our answering machine. She's coming to get Giselle for the picnic. They'll get to watch the sunset together.

Owen is in the kitchen. I give him two Popsicles.

One for Tommy.

He's gone.

Back to his parents?

Nope.

Where?

Someone else's house.

Whose house?

Don't know.

Is he coming back here?

Don't know.

Is he all right do you think?

I don't know.

How do you feel about it?

Owen shrugs, turns the radio up.

On the mirror of my dresser is a photograph of a family barbecue taken just a few days before, at Wayne's sister's. Jill is in a white sailor cap, a navy ribbon on the brim, and a white dress, stiff as a fresh piece of paper. She's sitting on Wayne's lap. Owen wears a skewed baseball cap, has a hotdog in his mouth, burly shoulders. Behind them, out of focus, is Giselle, her body arched backwards in a paroxysm of laughter. A potato chip in her fingers. She's holding it in the air as if the chip will save her from falling into an epilepsy of joy, the way a slapstick comedian totters and reels all over the stage with a full wine glass, not spilling a drop. A strand of her hair is loose on her cheek, a Hawaiian shirt, too big for her. Behind her, the shrubbery is dark, wet from the sprinkler, cave-like, something she could suddenly get up and walk into, disappear.

I stare at the photograph, at everyone laughing, the aura of summer heat at dusk. I try to remember if the afternoon was as carefree as it seems. Even if the camera couldn't capture all the detail (the white kittens in the shade of the blue fir, the heat making a soft mist around the red Chinese lanterns) it seems our happiness is exaggerated. That first line from *Anna Karenina*; each family is unhappy after its own fashion.

Giselle is coming from her mother's tonight. She's always upset when she leaves her mother's. Wayne and I will read in the study and listen to her trying to cry quietly. The sharp intake of breath, the way it chuffles out. One of us will go in and smooth her hair, the pillow hot, damp. One year her mother lived only a few streets away, and Giselle could see one of her windows from our third floor. Giselle would phone her mother each night before bed, standing in the window facing the lit square a few streets away. Talking to it. I'm afraid of whatever pain adolescence will bring her. I'd stop it if I could, like the King and

Queen in "Sleeping Beauty," banishing all the spinning wheels in the kingdom, trying to outwit fate.

The rain is spitting off the street, running in plaited streams down the pavement. The door bell rings. I put my eye to the peephole, press my forehead against the steel door. Giselle is here early. She steps back onto the street. The fisheye glass makes the street lurch behind her, the clapboard houses bowing around her like a rib cage after a sharp breath. She stands with her face turned up to the rain. She stands like that for a moment, then raises her arms, palms up. The rain comes down stronger when she lifts her arms. I can hear it in the drainpipe on the concrete step, like a jackhammer. I feel the thunder through the skin of my forehead against the cool steel. Giselle stands in the centre of the peephole. When the lightning flickers, I am the one who flinches.

Purgatory's Wild Kingdom

Julian is thinking about the woman and child he left in Newfoundland when he moved to Toronto. He's remembering Olivia preparing him a sardine sandwich, the way she pressed the extra oil out of each sardine on a piece of paper towel. Then she cut the head and tail off, each sardine, until they were laid carefully on the bread. Her head was bent over the cutting board. Her blond hair slid from behind her ear. He could see the sun sawing on her gold necklace. The chain stuck on her skin in a twisty path that made him realize how hot it was in the apartment. She was wearing a flannel pajama top and nothing else, a coffee-coloured birthmark on her thigh, shaped like the boot of Italy. Eight years ago.

Julian is sitting at the kitchen table with a pot of coffee. His bare feet are drawn up on the chair, his knees pressed into the edge of the table. It's a wooden table top that has been rubbed with linseed oil. There are scars from the burning cigarettes his wife occasionally leaves lying around. Small black ovals. There are thousands of knife cuts that cross over each other like the lines on a palm. He runs his finger over the table, tracing the grain of the wood. He pours another cup of coffee, and glances at the phone. Sometimes the university calls for Marika before nine, although they have been told not to. Marika requires only seven hours' sleep, but if she's disturbed she's tired all day. She wakes up at exactly nine every morning. She's proud of the precision of her inner clock. Julian likes to pick up the phone before it rings twice. Lately, when the phone rings and Julian answers, nobody speaks.

Marika is fifteen years older than Julian. The people on this street are very rich. The brick houses are massive. Some of them have been broken into apartments and rented. There's almost no traffic. The trees block most of the noise. He and Marika don't know their neighbours. Once, while out taking photographs, Julian met a man three houses up who was riding a sparkling black bike in circles. The man said he was Joe Murphy. Joe Murphy's Chips sold a large percentage of their product in Newfoundland. He gave the silver bicycle bell two sharp rings.

"The bike's a birthday present from my wife. It's a real beauty, isn't it?"

The trees shivered suddenly with wind and sloshed the bike with rippling shadows. Joe Murphy was wearing a suit and tie. The balls of his feet pressed against the pavement and there were sharp little crevices in his shined leather shoes. A crow left a tree and flew straight down the centre of the street. Julian lifted his camera and took a picture of Joe Murphy. In the far distant corner of the frame is the crow. Joe Murphy is out of focus, a blur in the centre of the picture, his face full of slack features. The crow is sharp and black.

"That makes me very uncomfortable," said Joe Murphy. "I think you have a nerve." He gave the bell another sharp ring, and pushed off the curb. His suit jacket flapping.

For two years, Julian has been sleeping a lot. It's taken him two years to fall away from any kind of sleeping pattern. This way he's always awake at different hours. This seems exotic to him, but the cost is that he can't will himself to sleep. He sleeps in the afternoon and then finds himself awake at four in the morning. At dawn he sometimes wanders around the neighbourhood. The light at dawn allows him to see straight into the front windows of the massive houses on their street, all the way to the back windows and into the backyards. It makes the houses seem like skeletons, with nothing hanging on the bones.

Sometimes Julian is asleep when Marika gets home from work. If there's no supper cooked for her she'll eat white bread and butter with spoonfuls of granulated sugar. Julian likes to cook for her and she likes what he cooks. But she's also happy to eat bread and sugar. She makes coffee and folds the bread and sinks it into her coffee. The soaked bread topples and she catches it in her mouth. The cats slink in from all the different rooms of the apartment and curl around her feet, or on her lap. She lifts the kitten and puts it inside her jacket. If Julian stumbles down the stairs, half awake, and he sees Marika bathed in the light of a fashion show on TV with her sugared bread, he feels that he has failed her. The failure makes him even sleepier. He can't keep his eyes open.

Marika is not one for dwelling on the past. Julian knows very little about her past. Not that she's secretive. It's the kind of conversation that bores her. Marika has a powerful charm. She's a chemistry professor, but most of her friends are artists or writers. At parties, for conversation, she offers crystallized stories about nature or the stars. If someone interrupts her to ask about her parents, or something back in France, she answers in short sentences, faltering.

She thinks of memory only as a muscle that must be exercised to keep the whole mind sharp. She is interested in sharpness. If asked, she can recall exactly what she did on any date two years before. She will remember what she wore, what Julian wore, what they ate, the content of any conversation that occurred on that day. But this is just a game.

Marika thinks about infinite tracts of time, about meteorology, about hummingbirds, about measuring the erosion of coastlines, and whether the continents could still lock together like a jigsaw puzzle, or a jaw grinding in sleep. She thinks about the Tower of Babel, or about fish that swim up the walls of fjords as if the walls were the lake bottom. What such swimming against the stream does to their skeletons. When she isn't thinking things like this, she watches soap operas, or drives in her car, or she and Julian make love.

Julian has watched Marika simulate theoretical galaxies on the computer. She has found this program mostly to amuse him. He has seen two galaxies blinking together, dragging their sluggish amorphous bodies toward each other across the black screen. Each blink represents a million years, until they pass through each other. The gravitational pull of each galaxy affects the shape of the other until some stars are clotted in the centre, and the rest spread on either side of the screen like giant butterfly wings. Marika has shown him thousands of things like this. She has described the path of the plague in the Middle Ages, drawing a map on a paper napkin at a donut shop. She told him that in Egypt they have found the preserved body of a louse, on the comb of Nefertiti. A drop of human blood, perhaps Nefertiti's blood, was contained in the abdomen of the louse. They have discovered many things about ancient disease from that drop of blood.

Julian collects the stories Marika tells him, although they often lose their scientific edges. He can't remember how old the louse was. For some reason the only thing he remembers about the plague is a medical costume, a long robe with the head of a bird. The doctor looked out through two holes cut in the black feathered hood, over a protruding beak.

When he is awake, Julian pursues the morals of these stories, something other than what lies on the surface. Just as he can't imagine how much time it took to create the universe from a black hole, he can't get at that hidden meaning.

Recently Marika contracted a virus that caused a nervous disorder. If not diagnosed, this disease can spread quickly through the body and destroy the tips of all nerve endings irreparably. It started with a numbness in Marika's left cheek. She had it checked immediately. Of course, she had access to the best medical care in Toronto. The disease was arrested before any serious damage was done, but the nerves in Marika's saliva ducts grew back connected to one of her tear ducts. Now when she eats her left eye waters.

Julian has begun to suspect that Marika doesn't talk about her past because she is afraid she will seem like an old woman. It was her eye, filling of its own accord, that started him thinking this way. The eye is the first sign of Marika's age. When her eye waters he's filled with fright. That fright causes its own involuntary response in him. He's remembering things he hasn't thought about in years. He has noticed that the skin on Marika's face looks older than before. The pores are larger. There are more wrinkles. The soft white pouches beneath her eyes are larger. That skin seems as vulnerable to him as the flesh of a pear he is about to bite.

He was going through their wedding photographs. Julian took them himself, so most of the pictures are of Marika. She is wearing a white silk jacket, cut like a lab coat, and the apartment is full of white blossoms. Her face looks so much younger that for a moment he has the feeling the photographs have been doctored.

They're eating a dinner of lamb and fresh mint. Marika's knife is whining back and forth on the dinner plate.

"Could you stop that noise?"

Marika's body jerks, as if she didn't realize he was sitting beside her.

"I was lost in thought. Thinking of crabs."

A tear is running down her cheek.

"In Guatemala," she says, "there's a species of crab that burrows into the ground and brings up in its claws shards of ancient pottery."

She lays down her knife and wipes a tear off her cheek with the back of her hand.

"The crabs descend beneath layer after layer to different cities that have been piled on top of each other, over time. Each city is hundreds of years younger than the one below it. The crabs mix the pottery shards together, all these ancient layers mixed together in the light of day. You really know very little about me. You know nothing about science."

Julian notices that both Marika's eyes are watering now and realizes she's crying.

In his dreams the stories Marika tells him are fables. He dreams about a crab that presents him with a jacket of glass shards that came from a wine bottle he once threw at Olivia. Olivia wears a cloak of stars. She opens her arms and the cloak is wrenched away from her, leaving her naked. She becomes two women, a blurred image, Marika and Olivia both.

That night Julian leaves the house at midnight and walks for hours. Outside the Royal Ontario Museum the moonlit gargoyles are covered with burlap bags, and look like robbers with nylon stockings over their faces. A group of five people dressed in cartoon costumes emerges from a church basement. They skip across the empty street and get into an idling mini-van. A man in a Pink Panther costume trails behind. He has removed the head of the costume and carries it under his arm. The man's own head looks abnormally small against the giant pink neck of the costume. Julian takes a picture of him.

Lately, Julian thinks about a memory lit with a big number one candle, a wax monkey wrapped around it. Julian carried the cake. He could feel the yellow of the flame under his chin, like the shadow of a buttercup. He could see his daughter's face buried in Olivia's blouse, both their party hats sticking off the sides of their heads. There was a blizzard outside and Julian felt like they were wrapped in white tissue paper. He left a few days after that. He hasn't spoken to either of them since.

Julian remembers things he didn't notice when they happened. He remembers a party in the country. Someone had shoved a hotdog wiener through a hole in a screen door, and every time the door slammed the hotdog wagged obscenely. It was the night he met Olivia. At midnight everyone went skinny dipping, the sound of diving bodies swallowed by the dark water. He was drunk and naked. When it came time to get out of the water he suddenly felt embarrassed. He asked Olivia to give him a hand, so he could hold a towel in front of himself. When she did haul him out he managed to drop the towel and got caught in the skittering path of a flashlight.

When Julian gets home from his walk he finds Marika asleep on the couch, a bowl of chips resting on her knee. She has fallen asleep in the middle of the night with her wrist hanging over the rim of the chrome chip bowl. The phone is ringing. Julian nearly trips over one of the cats in his rush to get it. It's ringing near Marika's ear. She doesn't stir.

⌒

Olivia's heels click down the hall through the loose pools of fluorescent light. It's Monday and the Topsail Cinemas mall is mostly deserted, except for the games arcade which shoots out synchronized pings and buzzes. Most of the stores have been in various stages of renovation all winter. Someone has been going at a cement wall with a jackhammer. Chunks of cement have fallen away and rusted bars stick out.

When Olivia turns the corner she sees the exhibit by a taxidermist from British Columbia named Harold. He's standing next to a chair, one hand on his hip, his index fingers looped through his change apron. When he sees Olivia he becomes animated.

"Step this way beautiful, beautiful lady. Let me take you on a whirlwind tour of purgatory's wild kingdom. Here you will see beasts miraculously wrested from the claws of decay. They have looked death in the eye. They have been consumed by death, but they are not dust. Thanks to the strange alchemy of embalming fluid and my own artistic wizardry, they live. They live."

He does this with a little flourish of his hands and a slight bow. Then he sighs as if he has used up all his energy. Pinching his nose, he says, "Two-fifty if you want to see it."

Olivia is twenty minutes early for the movie, so she says, "Sure, I'll treat myself, why not, it's my birthday."

Harold has a thick mop of black hair with silver at the sides; his body is very tall and thin. One of his eyes is lazy, straying off to the side.

The display takes the shape of a mini-labyrinth made of ordinary office dividers. At each turn the viewer comes upon another stuffed animal.

"Most of them are from endangered species. But the truly unique thing about this exhibit is that these animals have all been hit by trucks. Trucks or cars. Every one of them. Please don't think I would ever hurt these animals for the sake of the collection. I collect them only after they have been killed.

"I'm different from those taxidermists you see on the side of the road during the summer, of course. I've seen them in this province, in Quebec and Alberta as well, lined up in roadside flea markets next to tables that display dolls with skirts that cover toilet paper rolls. Those guys have a few birds, maybe, a couple of squirrels mounted on sticks, a few moose heads in the back of the station wagon. I take my work seriously. I'm always trying to get a lively posture."

Olivia has stopped in front of a moose. The moose is making an ungainly leap over a convincingly weathered fence, one end of which had been neatly sawed off for the purposes of the exhibit. The moose is raised on its hind legs. Its head and neck are hunched into its shoulders, as if it were being reprimanded.

"This moose looks funny."

Harold points to the neck, saying, "A less experienced man might have stretched the neck forward, and if I wished to be true to a moose in this position, that's what I would have done. I took this artistic license with the moose because it died on the hood of a station wagon. The antenna of the car, unfortunately, entered its rectum and pierced the bowel twice, like a knitting needle. After that I felt this moose should be preserved in an attitude of shame."

"Are you serious?"

"I travel the continent with these animals, setting up in strip malls all over the United States and Canada. I have a license. It's educational. Ottawa pays me. I am very serious. People have to know what we are doing to our wild kingdom. I try to respect the animals as individual creatures. Every sentient being deserves respect. Some of these species may never roam the Earth again. They're dead, of course, but I have preserved them. My part is small, I guess. I'm like a red traffic light. That's how I see myself. I do my thing, I make them pause for a minute, before they march off into extinction. It's a chance to say goodbye. We can't forget what we've destroyed."

The last animal is a polar bear. The office dividers are set up so that you come upon it suddenly. Its head and forepaws tower over the divider, but Olivia has been looking at a stuffed mother skunk and suckling skunks on the floor. When she walks around the corner she almost bangs into the bear. The animal's coat is yellowed, its jaw wide.

"She scared you," chuckles Harold and he pats the bear's coat twice, as if it's the bear that needs reassurance.

"This polar bear is my drawing card. The only animal not hit by a truck. This bear was shot. It wandered into a small town here in Newfoundland. It had been trapped on an ice floe. Starved. Dangerous. A mother bear separated from her cub. At seven in the morning a woman was putting out her garbage. The bear chased her back into the house. There was only an aluminum screen door between them. She got her husband's shotgun and when the bear crumpled the aluminum door, just like a chip bag, she shot it in the throat."

Harold parts the fur of the bear's throat. He has to stand on tippy toes to do so. Olivia can see the black sizzled hole, the fur singed pink.

At the end of the hall Olivia can see the woman in the ticket booth for the movie theatres. There's just one woman on tonight, although the twin booth is also lit with flashing lights that circle the outline of the booths. The ticket woman has taken a Q-tip from her purse and is cleaning her ear.

"You have a truck outside?"

"Yes, an eighteen-wheeler."

"Would you consider joining me for a beer? I can give you my address and you can pick me up later. I have a daughter but I have a babysitter lined up for the evening. I was going out anyway."

Olivia has asked the taxidermist out for a beer because she suddenly feels sad about being alone on her birthday. She has an image of this man driving across an empty Saskatchewan high-way with these wild beasts frozen in attitudes of attack, stretched in frozen gallops in the back of his truck. He is the first person she has met in months who seems lonelier than she is. There's the chance he won't show up.

At the bar Olivia gets drunk very fast. Harold drinks the same bottle of beer most of the evening. At last call he buys himself another. He feels jumpy, excited. He's been on the road for six months and almost always finds himself eating in empty hotel restaurants where the waitress watches a miniature TV with an earphone so as not to disturb him.

Olivia is beautiful, Harold thinks. She's wearing a man's shirt of moss-coloured material, and grey leggings. When she walks to the bar he can see all the muscles in her long legs. She reminds him of a giraffe, graceful despite her drunkenness and the fact that her legs are too long for her. Harold is adept at recognizing different kinds of drunkenness. In some people it twists free something bitter, but Olivia is blossoming. Her cheeks are flushed, her s's are lisping against her large front teeth. She has been telling him about the father of her child.

"My memories are like those animals in the back of your truck. I can take them out and look at them, all but touch them. Today is my birthday. I'm thirty, but time hasn't moved at all since he left. I don't look any older. I'm just waiting, that's all. Do you know what I think? I think he'll be back. I know he will. I know how to get in touch with him if there's an emergency with Rose, our daughter. I've got the number in my bedside table. But I haven't called him since he left. I'm waiting until he comes to his senses. You know what I think? I think he's been enchanted by an ice queen. You know, a splinter of glass in his eye, but one of these days an unexpected tear is going get it out. He'll be back, don't you worry, Harold."

Suddenly Harold is seized with worry. He removes his glasses. He puts his hand over hers on the table.

"Be honest with me, now. Does it bother you that I have a wandering eye?"

Olivia lays down her beer glass and draws one knee up to her chest.

"At first it was strange. I didn't know which eye to look into."

"In some cultures it is thought to be auspicious. In some cultures it's a sign. I'd like very much to go home with you this evening."

Olivia looks into his eyes, first one, then the other. Without his glasses they look even stranger. They are flecked with gold, the lashes, long and black, like a girl's.

They are lying side by side in bed. Harold is already asleep, his cheek nuzzled into her armpit, her arm over her head. He insisted on bringing the polar bear into the bedroom. He said it was worth thousands of dollars. He couldn't afford to leave it in the truck. A gang of men in a Montreal parking lot had broken into the truck, which was empty at the time, but he hadn't yet gotten the lock replaced.

The steps to Olivia's apartment were icy and when they got to the top, both of them straining with the bear, it slipped and its head thunked down the fifteen steps, denting its cheek. This almost made Harold cry with frustration.

He said, "What an indecency for that poor creature, the most noble creature in the wild kingdom."

The thumping woke the babysitter, who had fallen asleep on the couch. She pulled on her coat and boots and helped them with the bear.

The cold sobered Olivia considerably. They are lying in bed talking, with all their clothes on except for their shoes. She says, "Harold, do you mind if we don't make love?" and he says, "Not at all," but he is very disappointed.

She talks more about the father of her child. She has glow-in-the-dark stars pasted onto the bedroom ceiling. When Harold removes his glasses, the galaxy blurs and it looks as though they are really sleeping under the milky way. While she talks he puts his hand under her shirt onto her belly. The warmth of it, the small movement as she breathes is so charged with unexpected pleasure that Harold becomes almost tearful. He can't trust his voice to speak, so he lies beside her silently. They both fall asleep.

Olivia's eight-year-old daughter, Rose, is awake in her bed, terrified. She heard the thumping of something large and dangerous on the stairs outside, and drunken laughter. She heard whispers from her mother's room. She makes herself small against the headboard of the bed. She sits there watching the door of her room, waiting for something terrible to bash it open. She watches the clock radio with the red digital numerals change, change, change. Then she gets out of bed. She creeps along the hall to her mother's room. The hall light is on. She squeezes the glass doorknob with her sweaty hand and slowly, so the hinges won't creak, pushes the door open. The light falls on the raging polar bear, frozen in the act of attacking her sleeping mother. Rose doesn't move. The bear doesn't move. Everything stays as it is for a long time until the man next to her mother raises himself up on his elbow and says, "Little girl?"

Rose slams the door and runs to the phone. She dials the number and it rings several times. She can hear her mother calling her. Then a man answers the phone. She says, "Daddy, is that you?"

Julian has been awake, although it is four in the morning. He has been sitting on the couch holding Marika's hand. He hasn't moved her or disturbed her in any way since he took the chip bowl from her, except to hold her hand. He says, "Yes, this is daddy."

He has been awake but it feels as if the child's voice has awoken him. He knows who she is but for a moment her name slips his mind. For a moment, he can not for the life of him remember it.

Granular

Carpet burns on my elbows, our skin smelling of pond water, mud. You part the lips of my vagina with your tongue licking summer dampness and my own clear sticky mucus. Your thumb rubs circles outside my vagina, slow idle circles like someone making the rim of a crystal glass whine with a wet finger. My skin is cold from swimming, like the skin of someone else. I get up and go to the kitchen, take a cucumber from the fridge and peel away the dark rubbery skin with a paring knife. Carol has taken Sally and Kyle to the park. The house is empty.

Greenish white flesh, a clammy spring smell. I lie flat on the bed in our room, my arms over my head, legs spread. You move the cucumber down the ridges of my neck, chest bone, circle one nipple, a shiny snail's trail down my belly. Icy on my clitoris, numbing. You hold it gently against the opening of my vagina. You lick my clitoris, hold it between your lips, suck it.

You shift so your penis hangs in my face; I rake my fingers down the backs of your thighs. I have to lift my head off the bed to take your penis in my mouth. You stop licking me just as I'm about to come, my spine arching stiff as a bridge, each vertebra locking like a keystone. You don't let me come. You push the cucumber inside me, shocking cold.

I suck your cock hard.

The phone rings. The phone rings.

We are statues, like in the children's game when the music turns off and everyone freezes. Then you put your mouth back on my clitoris and I come in long shudders, the cucumber dragging the orgasm longer, gritty like the trail of a wet towel in the sand. You put the cucumber in my mouth and I bite it, a burst of jelly and seeds. My foot cramps, stiff, surprised as a starfish out of water. You bellyflop onto my stomach, your penis deep in my vagina. I reach down and rub my clitoris; my gold rings clink together, a tiny sound between our wet bellies, digging my heels, I'm coming again.

When you're about to come all the muscles in your face draw down in a surprised grimace, your eyes open wide. You pull out of me, jerk yourself a few times so you come over my belly. That's our birth control. Our teeth kiss, awkward. We lie side by side on the bed.

Who do you think was on the phone? I say.

You say, Your mother.

Your mother, I say.

Did you have a good time?

Yes. Did you?

I had a very good time, did you?

Yes I did.

I pull the blanket over me. My arms are under the blanket and you sit up on your elbow. What are you doing?

Nothing. What do you think I'm doing?

Ellen, you weren't putting my sperm inside you, were you?

Jesus, Rob.

Were you?

No. I wasn't. What a thing to accuse me of.

Then I'm thinking about if I had. I'm thinking about all the possibilities that spring up every time we act, then fall away to be replaced with another set of possibilities. Sometimes the import of our actions catches up with us. Import settles on one thing or another, the rim of a coffee cup, for instance, like a butterfly.

Carol told her boyfriend for six years that if he didn't marry her she'd leave him. She got pregnant and left. She and the baby moved in with us. Her boyfriend knew the split was coming and didn't know. It was a possibility that existed simultaneously with the more likely possibility that Carol would never leave him. He wanted to marry her then, but it was too late. He'll never get over the loss. That happens sometimes, a loss is indelible.

If you left me I could never sleep beside someone else in the same way. It would be more like a business agreement. I'd be terse. Silly or not, I believe in this particular love. I'm sealing my fate.

Your mother said when you were five you went up to your waist in surf, holding a sandwich out of the water and a seagull snatched it out of your hand. You covered your eyes with your arm and the wings slapped your face. The seagull screeched, hovering, touching you repeatedly. When you looked, the sandwich was gone. I imagine that the seagull bestowed on you the gift of charm in the sandwich's stead, like a fairy godmother. Your charm is made of a kind of nerve and innocence. You trust people and it takes them by surprise. Your trust is an ambush.

I've thought about cheating on you only once. I hitch-hiked a ride with a stranger travelling through Alberta. The sun fell through the windshield into my lap.

He said, But I admire you, that you can have these crushes on other men and not be afraid of cheating on your husband. You admit the possibility exists, though? Look!

I looked and it was a field of rippling sunflowers. Vivid yellow. A transport truck flew past on the other side of the highway and our pick-up veered into its path. The man gave the wheel an involuntary jerk. The height of the transport truck, the chance of being crushed to death, the thought that sex with this man would be an isolated act, without consequence — the possibilities dispersed in waves of diminishing strength over the nodding heads of the sunflowers.

Squinting at the sun through my eyelashes. Splintered yellow petals. Vision as clear and potent as vodka. The vodka Carol's Bulgarian friend collected like sweat from the still he made by sealing a pot with a wreath of bread dough. Catching the drips, the pot vibrating on the orange element, frothing with a religious fervour, sweating a few drops into a cup. The Bulgarian pours some on the palm of his hand, and lights it with a match. A blue flame licks his palm like a dog's tongue. He holds it out, smiling, then — Ah ah ah ah! when the slick of alcohol burns off and the heat touches his palm, he shoos it like a pitched butterfly. Pssst. It's out.

I dream I'm lying naked on my stomach in the sand. The sun is hot, my skin just beginning to burn. You take a heavy paper bag, and begin to pour careful lines of sugar on my body. You begin with the bone of my heel. My toes dig in until they reach wet sand, the line of sugar continues up my calf, thigh, between the cheeks of my bum, up my spine. The sound of the sugar falling through the creases of the paper is as ticklish as the grains of sugar bouncing on my warm skin.

You say a word to me without moving your lips. One word that contains the Holy Grail, a key that will unlock me. You are communicating it at a huge sacrifice to yourself. The word becomes saturated with overwhelming love the way tea will creep into a spoonful of sugar if you dip just the tip of the spoon. The word is *granular*. As I'm drawn out of sleep I know I must hang onto the word, as if I'm holding the string of a kite, but as I draw it in, the meaning of the word is lost, just as chunks of the sky swoop away from a descending kite. I say the word *granular* in a whisper, then in an ordinary voice. I can't even think what the word usually means.

When I wake, you're practising the cello. The instrument

sounds drunken, losing the thread of its own thought. It takes me a while to recognize "Twinkle, Twinkle, Little Star." Someone in the house applauds. The geranium is straining toward the rain-pitted window. Then, a shower of four petals.

I sit on the toilet seat and talk, while you are in the bath, about a drive across the island. About a moose I'd seen on the side of the road, a small female that stood still at the edge of a pool. The pool was marbled with cloud, the moose golden in the six o'clock light, completely still.

You stand and the water makes a smacking noise like a big kiss. You take a towel and squeak the steam from the mirror. The hair on your legs is flattened with water, water seeping onto the linoleum around your feet.

I say, Get on the mat.

Breathing warm steam. Droplets form on my heavy sweater. I'm too lazy to lift my arms over my head to take it off.

You smooth shaving cream onto your face and neck, raise your lower lip up toward the ceiling, top lip crimped tight. Holding your neck with your thumb and forefinger, you stroke hard with the razor under your chin, jutting one side of your jawbone, then the other, toward the mirror, cream piled against razor like a snowplough. The bathroom window reflects in the steamy mirror. A crow lands on the telephone wire outside, and for a moment the wings seem to batter your head gently.

You rent a video camera for Sally's birthday. When the children have gone home we replay the afternoon. You with the cake. The camera sears a residue of candle light onto the tape, a bluish streak that floats over your shoulder like a streamer. The last line of "Happy Birthday" sounds almost melancholic, baritone. The other children, and their pointed party hats and kazoos, become brownish silhouettes as Sally bends over the cake. Her lips gleam. Her crimson cheeks can't get enough breath to blow out the candles, the flames like punching clowns bouncing back, gilding her tangled hair.

In the evening I come into the bedroom and you've set up the monitor with the video camera pointed at the bed. The room on the screen is hot, yellowish, textured with fuzzy dots. I take off my clothes. You zoom in tight so my skin fills the screen like sand dunes. You zoom out and I turn my bum toward the camera, lift my leg. I turn myself every way. You take off your clothes and sit down beside me. The molecules of our skin are vibrating.

You say, I'll do something about the colour.

I like the colour.

Tentatively, we touch each other, watching the screen. It takes a second for my hand to find you because you are closer than you appear.

I say, Is this thing running?

You say, Let's tape it, we'll erase it after.

At first the whir of the camera fills the room. You press my legs open in the direction of the lens, watching the monitor over your shoulder.

Then we make love, forgetting the camera.

Afterwards we watch it. For a long time you were bent with your head between my legs, the skin of your back shimmering. The only movement visible for several minutes is my knee entering the screen slowly and dropping away. Then my arms come up around your hips, move over your hips, my fingers spread on your back. It looks like a varnished oil painting, age disintegrating the image.

Our sex broken down into grains of pure colour, drawn through the blue eye of the camera, a private constellation of us, sticking to the magnetic tape. No sound.

You say, It comes from having sex with the same person for so long. That gentleness.

Walking up Victoria Street at night, headlights separate my shadow into several separate bodies that drop away from each other like a chain of paper dolls joined at the hands, all sliding sideways over each other, over the clapboard. The car roaring uphill and zooming away, the silhouettes becoming one at the toes of my shoes. All the possibilities coming into existence and dropping away with each step.

I think of having another baby. Perhaps our life would spill over. Perhaps we could no longer contain our life. Today I dropped Sally at day care and she cried to break her heart. I had to pry her fingers off my leather jacket to run out the door. But then I think, in the future I'll regret not having another child. I will not understand whatever crooked path of thought led me to deciding I didn't want another one.

Carol's laughter is like spraying champagne suppressed by a thumb. It's her turn to cook. She's in the kitchen beneath us dancing the knife over the onions, toe-heel-toe-heel. Slow first, like Anthony Quinn in *Zorba the Greek*, then faster, red pepper, banana pepper, the seeds burning her lips, the cleaver juicy. The onions slip into the hot oil.

There you are in the mirror of the wardrobe, the door swinging open. Milky light flashing over you like a waterfall. You bend one knee coyly, cover your genitals with your hands, mock femininity. The light rippling over your white long limbs. You're standing in a giant clamshell of laundry. You turn from the mirror with a big bobbing cock.

From the window I can look down on the back yard. Sally and some friends run through the front door — slam — the paddywhacks of their feet slapping the linoleum — slam — the back door, squeals with the garden sprinkler, they've turned on the sprinkler — like the giant feather fans eunuchs wield in old Hollywood movies about harems. Beads of silvery light, some red, some blue, languidly swaying on the children — Sally, three, is naked, except for the fur of cut grass that has stuck from the waist down, half goat/half child. The wind lifts her purple straw hat an inch off her head, it's tied under her chin. You've cut my initials in the grass with the lawn mower, big block letters. Sally dives into the Big Bird wading pool, it makes a yellow blush on her body, like when you hold a buttercup under your chin. She splits the stagnant skin of water, dead bugs, cut grass. I want another child. Do you hear me? Soon it will be too cold for the sprinkler.

Downstairs the kettle whistles and Carol tells Kyle to wash his feet under the hose before he comes in. Carol has formed herself around her son the way a pearl grows around a grain of sand. Kyle has become handsome. His skin is dusky, a mole on his cheek, thick sooty lashes. Carol's told me this story more than once. She noticed the silence behind her. She turned, her wrist falling loose with the knife. There was Kyle with a plastic bag over his head, an egg of hollow plastic drawn into his mouth, his face blue, blue. She thought he was already dead because he wasn't moving.

She holds her hands out in front of her, elbows on the table, gargoyle claws.

I clawed it off his face, she says. I clawed it off. Tears start in the corners of her eyes. Her hands are still out in front of her. She draws them back, laughs, rubs them together.

Sometimes when we are having sex, a lost afternoon from months ago, or years, will creep over my skin. It's visceral, the way a flatfish draws shades and patterns from the sand it floats over. Grainy blushes, they're gone before I can speak them.

That perfume salesman in Toronto, crouching at the corner of Yonge and Bloor. He's talking, opening cases, a loose crowd tightening around him like a shrinking sweater. He rips the lid off a stolen carton; inside, the dark gold bottles sit in cardboard pockets, like honey in a honey comb. The weave of the crowd is tight as tweed, his pants are tight across the muscles of his thighs. His shoes squeak, you can see the teeth marks of the comb in his thick, oiled black hair. Then two cops are pushing through the crowd, half jogging through the traffic. The crowd turns back to the perfume salesman, but the circle of sidewalk where he was standing is empty, as if we had gathered tight around a lost possibility. That afternoon comes to me, we had walked all day, the wind making our cheeks smart. I want to grab your wrists and say, What afternoon am I thinking of? I'm convinced you'd know.

Or you would say, Sally standing on a chair wiping wide circles of condensation from the patio window. Mommy, make me a pumpkin. Her palm squeaking against the glass, the erased circle of condensation forming a halo around her. A wet slice of her red tricycle through the wiggly finger trails on the glass. Shrivelled pumpkins, their mouths puckered as if they have lost their teeth.

I catch the waterfall of mirror as the door swings and you're standing in a pile of laundry, naked, your cock standing out from your body. The sun is sinking red, and when I turn from the window the room seems dark. The wardrobe door winches like splintering wood, dry wood cracked over a knee. The day is over.

I'm sitting with a cup of cold coffee. Your cock bobs, you walk right over and stick it in my mouth, your hand gentle on the back of my hair. There's a stirring in the corner of the room. A panting. It's the husky. The white husky we're taking care of for the neighbours. We're startled to stillness but the dog gets to its feet, an ovation, its pink tongue, thirsty. When your come — slam — the back door — Jesus you've got water all over the floor — hits the back of my — slam the front door —

throat, I'm still holding the coffee cup in the air, prissy, stiff, as if a waiter will come by to fill it.

I turn my head and the sun is down now, down. A red ray comes through the window and catches in the edges of the husky's coat. Gold nettles and burrs are snagged in his white fur as if he has been galloping, chasing through the underbrush of our sex.

Ingrid Catching Snowflakes on Her Tongue

Ingrid moves around the kitchen. The shadows of the leaves flow over her like a home movie; the shadows on the linoleum lap at the toes of her boots. The cutlery rattles. She's laying down forks and knives. I'm putting down plates. My husband, Mike, and Ingrid used to live together. They were together for three years. They were both single parents when they met, barely twenty. But I knew her before he did. I've just remembered this. I knew her, from a distance, in the summer of grade five, before anything had happened to either of them.

She was the girl in the yellow bathing suit. Competitive water-skiing. I'd seen her take the ramp. I didn't know her name, but I knew who she was. Her yellow suit would shoot off the ramp, an erratic jerk, as she caught her balance. She could make everybody's stomach lift with her. The spank as she hit the water. A curt wave to everyone on the beach, cut short by a grab for the wooden handle. The guys in the boat went so fast they stippled the surface, making it like an unpaved road. She was as rigid and concentrated as a man with a jack-hammer.

I was afraid of water-skiing so my parents bought me Jesus boots. A giant Styrofoam boat for each foot. Bungling to a standing position, my legs slipping away from each other, I'd catch Ingrid out of the corner of my eye. On the other side of the lake she was so small she seemed to be standing still, loitering.

Now she smokes, is languid. Her chuckle is like cola pouring from a plastic bottle. But she still has an athlete's body, angular, broad-shouldered, lean.

Once, when she was in the bath, she flexed the muscles in her leg for me, the water slurping as she lifted her leg straight into the air and moved her fingers down the back of her thigh.

"These muscles are my favourite, see the definition?"

I could see three ripples, drops criss-crossing through the wiry gold hair on her calves.

She had glued seashells around the edge of the old-fashioned tub. A mask, snorkel and flippers hung from the pipes. Three melon scented candles made the steam as yellow as smoke. Several squares of coloured glass lined the window ledge.

The coloured glass is from the apartment on Jasper Street where Ingrid lived when my husband was in love with her. It was no small love, I know that much. Sometimes when she's visiting, my throat constricts with jealousy. It's not that I think they're still in love. I'm jealous of when they were.

I like sitting on the staircase listening to our house. The gravelly voice of the coffee maker in the kitchen, something metal turning over in the dryer, the ebbing of canned laughter from behind a bedroom door on the third floor. Mike's daughter Mary rubbing against the tub, flaccid splashes. The house is a skeleton and our moods surge along the wiring, spilling through the pipes, circulating like currents of heat. Living under the same roof with someone else shapes you both, the way liquid takes the shape of its container.

Ingrid's old apartment building on Jasper Street was demolished recently. I was there when the construction workers started. The face was pried away; it fell onto the street with a ringing slap. The other walls were left standing for a while. Rain streamed down the wallpaper; seals with beachballs in Gabe's room, raised velvet in Ingrid's.

It was like a theatre set. I stood on the sidewalk, listening to the rain drum on a doorless fridge. I thought of the noises that used to be there — vegetables sliding into hot cooking oil, magnetic letters slipping down the fridge door when it slammed, her rowing machine, Mike's typewriter, the scratchy needle on the record player, the sound of their sex.

My husband had a new daughter, Mary. He was taking her for three days a week. You could see your breath on cold days in the apartment. The wiring was dangerous. Ingrid and Mike put plastic over all the windows, holding a hair dryer over it to shrink it tight. A trace of kerosene in the air from the heater they dragged from room to room.

Mike's told me that sometimes the babies cried all night, Mary starting to cry when Gabe was finally exhausted. Mike's only escape was to take a bath. Or he would go to the corner store, lean on the freezer holding a slice of bologna in wax paper, and watch the snow fall.

He'd put Gabe and Mary in his eiderdown army jacket and zip it up. They'd sleep like that, Gabe's blond curls tangled with Mary's straight black hair.

Once both the children were playing on the kitchen floor while Mike was chopping turnip. He lifted the knife dramatically over his shoulder and the blade flew out and stuck in the cupboard between the children's heads. Another time a garbage truck backed over the children's toboggan, just as Gabriel had rolled away from it, crushing the curved wooden lip under the back tires. The children would often bite each other until they broke the skin. Ingrid breast fed Gabriel even after he was able to ask for booby. Sometimes she breast fed Mary.

When Ingrid drops by and Mike is in the kitchen, sometimes they'll talk about these memories and shake their heads with quiet astonishment. When they talk about that time they become almost shy of each other.

I go up to the bathroom to make sure Mary has rinsed all the shampoo out. Her hair is pressed against the water like licorice ropes in a glass jar, her body submerged to the neck in the shallow bath, her eyes closed. She looks like Snow White in the glass casket. For the first time I see her breasts are growing, small buds. Without opening her eyes she crosses her arms over her chest and says, "What do you think you're staring at?"

I bend a strip of the venetian blind, clear a spy hole in the condensation with my finger. Mike is coming down the street with an armload of groceries.

Ingrid concealed her pregnancy. She was working in a second-hand bookstore. One day she didn't show up for work, the next day she came in with a baby boy. No one had guessed. No one knew who the father was, there weren't even any rumours.

She doesn't talk about her family much. They live in Alberta and they haven't spoken to her since Gabriel was born. Ingrid's careful with the small amount of money she lives on. She buys things rarely, but when she does it's something that will last. Quality. An English duffle coat of navy felt with bone buttons for Gabe. A cutlery set with heavy mother of pearl handles she found in a second-hand shop. Sometimes two months or more will go by when she can't pay the rent. She's been evicted. Has had her heat cut off. On winter nights we've gone for long walks and she's pointed out places she has lived in.

I imagine her standing on the doorstep of her parents' house, knowing she was pregnant. No money. I imagine it like the moment in the air when you leave the water-ski ramp, your stomach flipping up, being completely still and flying at the same time. I don't know where she could have gotten the courage. The first time you feel a baby move inside you, it's like

a candle flame, not the heat of the flame but its chaotic flickering in a draft. It's about the size of a flame and as frantic. If you
could hold a flame in your fist. You feel it over the pelvic bone
and immediately doubt that you've felt it. She must have
decided not to tell anyone, not even the father. That movement inside her, that's the only thing I can imagine giving her
the courage to leave her parents' house. November, with the
streetlights coming on, the branches bowed down with ice.

For some reason she started seeing Marcel, Gabriel's father,
again when Gabe was five. He stayed a month. It ended when
he took a swing at her. He's a small guy and he was drunk. She
hit him back and he fell onto his bum, his legs straight in front
of him, his toes pointing toward the ceiling, his palms flat on
the floor — like a kid at the beach, she said, sitting at the edge
of the sea. She knocked his glasses off and he blinked, slightly
sobered.

Mary was eight when Mike and I had a daughter of our
own. Mary stood over me, watching Jenny breast feed. She
tucked my hair behind my ear. "What does it taste like?" I
hadn't tasted it myself. I hate milk. Mike said he had tasted it
before. Ingrid's. Mary said in baby talk, "I want some." The
book said that if an older sibling shows curiosity, offer her
some. After a few squirts of milk she'll be bored with it. Mary
sucked my nipple. I felt the sharp tug all through my breast and
stomach, the touch of her teeth, rather than gums, harder than

my baby's suck. One squirt was enough. "Moo," she giggled, and was gone out of the room. With Mary, I sometimes feel that I'm pouring my love into a vacuum.

Sometimes when Mike and I have sex my mind races. The kind of kinetic energy that the shadows of the leaves have in that reflected murky square on the wall. The leaves are as sharp as characters of the alphabet, but they move over each other, disintegrate before they can spell anything. Sounds, smells, images, every sensation slipping over the next, chaotic, ticklish. I can feel the metallic yelp of the mailbox lid at the tips of my teeth and I have to run my tongue over them. The smell of ink, like the smell of blood. A fingernail broken to the quick, rubbed against a cotton bed sheet. Then the smell of paint thinner.

Paint thinner on the back deck in a plastic tub. A week ago I lifted the lid, then noticed Ingrid walking back from Carnell's store. I could just see her through the alley between the opposite houses. She was weighed down with grocery bags, Gabriel scuffing behind her. She had to stop for a rest. I could imagine the plastic handles cutting into her fingers. She was under a streetlight and she stuck her tongue out. It had started to snow, an early November snow. She was catching snowflakes on her tongue.

In the middle of sex I mix her up with vapours from the paint thinner, how they evaporate in the air, like home-made vodka, or barbecue starter, nail polish remover. I was afraid there might be a time in the future when she wouldn't be as important to me as she is now. When I might not know her.

Just as I'm about to come, I feel her on the edges of my teeth too, and I almost say out loud in Mike's ear, "Ingrid's coming for supper."

Mike sometimes wakes and says he's just had an erotic dream. They can be about anyone, but they're often about Ingrid. "What happens?"

"What do you mean?" he says, "We were screwing, it was really nice."

I ask Mike where his dreams happen. Do they have sex on damp concrete floors in the basements of strange buildings, or in a dory that's heading through the Narrows, are there knives or vegetables or candles in the dreams? He says no, there's just his body and Ingrid's and intense physical pleasure.

Ingrid was visiting the first time I clipped Jenny's fingernails. A nurse at the hospital had told me to bite them off, but I was using the clippers. Ingrid was washing the dishes. I sliced the top of Jenny's finger off. The little knob of flesh sticking to the tip of the nail clipper. I held Jenny out in my stiff arms. For a long time she didn't draw a breath, her face got redder and redder, her mouth stretched open. Then, as if to make her get on with it, I screamed myself. Ingrid turned from the sink and took Jenny from me. The blood drenched Jenny's sleeper, smeared over Ingrid's cheeks. It soaked a thick face cloth, then a dishtowel. I followed Ingrid to the bathroom, blood dripping on each step. Both my fists clenched over my mouth. Ingrid filled the tub and put Jenny in. The water turned pink, then red. The finger spurted for fifteen minutes. The strength of my scream and a tingle in my arms from holding them so tight to my chest made me fill up with calm, like a glass of cold water.

When Mike got home I kissed him in front of Ingrid, something I never do. He smelled of yeast, poppy seeds; his mouth tasted of coffee, honey and cigarettes. He saw the stiffened sleeper on top of the garbage. Ingrid had turned to look out the window.

This is what I know about Marcel, Gabriel's father. Ingrid said it was a one-night stand.

When I was seventeen, Marcel was thirty. A photographer. He lived in a house out in the Battery, by himself. The living room made up most of the house. One giant plate of glass looked over the harbour, into the city. At night the city was just orange and white lights. They licked the land like a fire that breathes in a wood chunk, with no flame. Sometimes they spread a flicker over the whole city like a shiver on a horse's flank.

Marcel's fridge was full of photographic paper and chemicals. Bottles of liquor, wine. A bottle shaped like a Spanish dancer. No food. He ate out, always. The front door didn't close properly, he had to lean a car tire against it to keep it from blowing open. If we were lying on his bed we would know if someone came in by the wobbling tire, the circles getting tighter and tighter. When he left the house it was padlocked shut. It never occurred to me to wonder where he got his money. He was silent about where he came from, except to say Toronto. He liked to dress in white. All white, including his socks, shoes, even his underwear, always. But wore black sunglasses.

Marcel's pictures were full of geometric shadows. Everything was balanced, contrived, mannered.

There's a photograph of himself in a room, empty of furniture except for a piano. He's wearing a white tuxedo, sitting with his back to the camera. A naked girl, sixteen, lies across the piano top looking into the camera — two cognac glasses. He usually made a point of staying out of photographs himself. This picture of his back was the only exception.

I heard Marcel talking about the girl. Ingrid. I remembered the name because I didn't know any Ingrids. He had the phone pinched between his ear and shoulder, he was swishing a shiny piece of paper in chemicals with a set of tongs. Even in black and white you could tell her pubic hair was gold. They must have been talking about it because I could hear his friend say through the receiver, "I like to get them young, then shave their pubic hair."

Marcel said, "I like to get them before they have pubic hair."

He hung up and pinned the photograph to a clothesline strung across the darkroom. There were ten other prints of the same picture. He was a fanatic about lint or dust, graininess.

I said, "I don't see how you could sleep with someone who was sixteen."

He said, "You're seventeen."

I didn't say anything to that. We hadn't had sex yet, not exactly. He hadn't photographed me naked either.

My mother showed up, and dragged me away. I was stinking of licorice.

He made the Pernod viscous, milky, by adding water. He had teased me into taking it in my mouth but I wouldn't swallow it. He dipped his tongue in my shot glass and licked it down the ridges of my throat. I could feel it cool, evaporating. I swallowed. The first time I had ever drunk alcohol. In an hour, I drank most of the bottle.

Marcel led me to the couch. He bit my tongue so hard he cut it on both sides.

My mother hit her horn at that exact moment. It might not have been the exact moment. It took a while for my mother's horn to burn through the Pernod. The lights were off in his house. I don't know how she knew I was there.

I stood up and tried to button my shirt, banged my shin on the corner of the coffee table, a shard of pain. I had a hard time moving the tire out of the way. It was as though photographing Ingrid was what made her pregnant. Nobody gets pregnant from a one-night stand.

In my mother's car, my body was shivering from drinking so much. I was poisoned. It was like the one time I tried to water-ski. I forgot to let go of the rope when I fell. Currents of water ploughing my gritted teeth. Dragged until I thought I would drown. Her horn was a simple sound, like a voice finally coming through the throbbing of an outboard motor, underwater. A wobbled voice, almost in another language, until the simplicity hits and you think you knew what it meant all along. Let go of the rope, stupid. Or: that's my mother outside, get off me, that's my mother.

It struck me he might have gotten the bottles mixed up, poured developing chemicals into me. All those Ingrids spilling off the black piano top like milky licorice in my mouth.

The Lonely Goatherd

The houses dig their heels into the hill to stop from tumbling into the harbour. The clapboard faces are stained with last night's rain. Everything is squeezed together and sad. Carl loves Anita but lately he's been sleeping with other women. It's not idiosyncrasies he's been sleeping with, it's bones. Cheek bones, hip bones, knees. He sees inside apartments of St. John's he will never see again.

Two nights ago he was in an apartment over Gulliver's Taxi Stand. The girl's stereo speaker picked up radio messages of the dispatcher. At about four in the morning Carl heard the taxi driver say, Sure that's only your imagination, almost as if he were tangled in the bed sheets with them. Carl felt like a kid.

The sad thing is Anita's art. She is painting golf courses from the TV set. The old man she nurses watches golf, tapes it with his VCR. She takes Polaroid snapshots of the screen. She wants to capture in her paintings the glossy finish of the

Polaroid, the snowy texture of the video, the play of light on
the manicured lawns, and the slow motion time of the ball flying through the air. She says it's an analytical reduction she's
after, always keeping herself distanced from the subject. They
don't talk about their problem, but when he looks at her paintings he feels she is stripping him like an onion, layer by layer,
her eyes watering.

Carl works at the Arts and Culture Centre, building sets. He
makes an adequate living working chiefly with Styrofoam. This
week he is building sets for a fairy tale amusement park. He
shows his own sculpture once a year.

A sea of white Styrofoam beads covers the floor, clings to
his pants, his bald head, and sticks to his hands like warts.
Thumb-tacked on the wall are several eighteenth century fairy
tale illustrations, before illustration got cute. Red Riding Hood
in the gnarled forest, eyes wide, the wolf, saliva drooling from
his fangs. Where Red Riding Hood's cape parts you glimpse a
white vulnerable breast. Carl flicks his pocket knife into the
illustration like a dart. Carl has been provided with an assistant
from the Student Employment Office. The assistant studies day
care management. Her name is Sarah. She is about ten years
younger than Carl, and is now sweating in her paper suit over
the giant chunk of Styrofoam from which the wolf will be
carved.

Anita found out she was pregnant the same time she took the
job nursing Mr. Crawhall. He sleeps most of the time she's
there. This gives her an opportunity to paint. The house is on

Circular Road, surrounded by trees which block the sound of traffic. Toward the end of the first week with Mr. Crawhall she entered the house and was assaulted by a loud consistent buzzing. She thought it was the buzzer by his bed, that Mr. Crawhall had died and his hand had fallen on the buzzer, but it was the egg timer on the stove. She has to serve him a three-and-a-half-minute egg every day. Her fingers shake a little on the silver teaspoon when she brings it near his mouth. It's different from feeding a baby, there's the question of Mr. Crawhall's dignity. Because of her condition the egg makes her nauseous. Once a hairline crack ran down the side of the egg and yolk seeped through it over the gold rimmed egg cup down to the saucer, threatening Mr. Crawhall's thin white bread. He said quite slowly, with his hands squeezed in the effort to speak, Oh, how have we managed to waste all that lovely yellow yolk?

Anita thinks of painting the egg as seen from under Mr. Crawhall's magnifying glass, but the jelly of it and the overt symbolism make her sick. She's planning an abortion. The baby isn't Carl's.

Sarah, the assistant, is more of a hindrance than a help. Her professional opinion after six weeks in day care training is that Carl is making fairy tale props too realistic. The Momma Bear and Poppa Bear look like real bears. Strands of melted clear plastic hang from their teeth. She says they'll have a damaging psychological effect. She feels fairy tales are violent and sexist. She thinks we should ship loads of grain to India, she talks about

McDonald's hamburger containers polluting the environment, American aggression in Nicaragua, and acid rain. Carl is building a cage for her out of two-by-fours and plastic sheeting so she can work with contact cement and the fumes will be contained within the cage. He gives her a gas mask, tightening the rubber strap around her fine hair. He puts her in the cage with one of the wolves. It's impossible to talk with a gas mask on. The rest of the afternoon the studio is quiet, except for the chain saw.

Anita watches *The Sound of Music* with Mr. Crawhall. He tells her to fast forward over the scene with Liesl and her boyfriend in the gazebo where she sings *I am sixteen going on seventeen, innocent as a lamb.* This scene bores Mr. Crawhall, so they watch it in fast forward. The dance number changes Liesl into a maddened butterfly batting the wings of her white skirt against the boy's head. She circles round and round him, flinging her arms this way and that, trapped in the amorphous white cloud. Her face in the close-up is contorted and pulled like plastic across the jiggling screen. When Anita presses "play," Julie Andrews sings, *These are a few of my favourite things.*

When Carl gets round to asking Sarah to sleep with him he tells her he is bored sleeping with his wife. Sarah asks, Is she intelligent?

Carl says, Yes, of course, she's a very articulate woman.

Does her conversation bore you? asks Sarah.

No, I love her.

Then I don't see why she should bore you in bed.

Well, her conversation might bore me if she were the only woman I had a conversation with in seven years.

He says after a moment, Don't worry about Anita; she gets it whenever she wants it. She has no idea how I feel.

Although Sarah feigns moral indignation, Carl feels her going soft like butter. She blushes when he compliments her and enjoys the special attention she gets around the workshop.

Mr. Crawhall's house is designed to allow as much sunlight as possible. When he's asleep Anita watches a white chair with faint apricot flowers. The shadows of the leaves on the chair are in constant motion. At about seven in the evening it's almost as though the chair catches fire, a silent fire. It's the only moving thing in the stiff-backed room besides the two goldfish. They are kept in a clear glass bowl with no plants or coloured stones. A soft spoken friend speaks to Anita over the phone, You really have no choice, Anita. This will hurt Carl so much. It was a one-night stand.

The goldfish are identical. Anita calls one fish the option of keeping the baby and the other the abortion. She watches them swim around and makes a game of seeing how long she can tell which is which.

That night Anita says to Carl, about her new painting, If you spend enough time alone the pain of emptiness passes and you realize your own voice is the only company you need.

The image is entirely nonrepresentational, red and yellow dots only, but the canvas shimmers with anxiety.

Carl tries to remember what it is he loves about Anita. The smell of turpentine on her flannel painting smock, burnt match sticks and beer bottle caps between the bed sheets. The squeezed paint tubes in her leather box, curled in on themselves, the limbs of their shirts and jeans twisted together on the floor. The photographs in his sock drawer, in the beaten Tooton's envelope, of the night they walked to Signal Hill. It was summer and the sky was a skin of ticklish rain. Anita was drinking pop that turned the down of her upper lip and tongue orange. She tasted like summer, childhood. In the photographs the lights of the city at night burned coloured sizzles on the film. They made love on the grass, watching out for broken beer bottles, an aureole of amber glitter around their bodies.

Anita slept with a tourist named Hans. He was a German gymnast who had trained for the Olympics for eleven years and gave it up. Now he was driving a VW van across Canada. St. John's was his starting point. He was golden, muscular, but small. He walked with his hands loosely by his sides. He seemed to place his steps, walking on the balls of his feet as if he were stepping onto a mat in front of a large audience. He had been sitting alone at the Ship Inn drinking milk. It was as though the blondness of his hair alarmed almost anyone who might have joined him. Hans and Anita discussed what was scenic, the hospitable Newfoundlander, and Jiggs dinner, briefly. He had come from California, that was his first stop in North America. He had learned to speak English in a place called Pure Springs, a self-awareness camp with hot springs where they practised

Gestalt and taught hyperventilation to relax. Hans talked about group therapy.

You are one of twenty-five for a month. You come to know each other very well and one day you step outside the room and the others decide on one word or a simple phrase that describes your essence. Sometimes it's very painful, but for the first time you see your true self. Everyone hugs and is supportive.

Anita asks, What was your word?

Cold fish.

Outside the Ship Inn a rusted sign pole stuck out from the brick wall. The sign itself had been removed. Hans climbed on the windowsill easily and, jumping, gripped the bar. He swung back and forth, then with his legs straight, toes pointed, lifted himself into a handstand. It was the moment while he was upside down that Anita realized she would sleep with him because he was passing through and because her faithfulness to Carl was a burden. When he swung down, Anita felt the pocket of warm night air he cut with his body.

Hans swept the seats of the VW van with a small hand brush before she got in. The van was spotless. There was a string bag full of fruit, none of it bruised. On the wall was a calendar from Pure Springs. The photograph for June was four pairs of naked feet, toes twisted, all caught in the same hammock net. Nestled between the hand-brake and the driver's seat was a glossy purple diary. Anita picked it up and opened it.

What's this?

Inside were poems written in German, diary entries, dried flowers, and coloured pencil drawings of mountain peaks.

My ex-fiancée made that for me.

Hans took out his shiny Swiss Army knife from the glove compartment and effortlessly cut the rind from a pineapple while he spoke, She was a gypsy. Long dark hair, black eyes, small like me, we wore each other's clothes. We hiked together in the mountains of Switzerland for two and three months at a time. We were together for ten years and were to be married. The invitations were sent. One hundred invitations. A week later she said she wanted to go to Africa. She met another fellow there, a German. The wedding was called off.

Hans held a quivering slice of pineapple out to Anita on the blade of the knife.

You must be very hurt, said Anita.

No, at Pure Springs they taught me to see myself as I really am. When I have finished my trip I will return there as a counsellor.

They sat in silence looking at the stars over Long Pond.

The fruit is very sour, remarked Hans. In the morning Anita could see the Arts and Culture Centre from where they had parked. She saw Carl get out of his car.

Hans dropped her off later at Mr. Crawhall's. When he left she could only imagine him in a hat with a little red feather, shorts with straps, and a walking stick; Julie Andrews's voice echoing off the Alps. *Such is the cry of the lonely goatherd la-he-o, la-he-o, dee-lo.*

It shocked her later to think her baby might be blond with eyes like an iceberg, if she had it.

Carl's troll is hunched under the bridge, naked, its long green fingers hanging between its knees. Carl is placing glass eyeballs in the carved eye sockets. Sarah is standing on a wooden chair, perfectly still, her pressed lips full of pins. She's modelling the Red Riding Hood costume for the seamstress. She's identical in size to the five Styrofoam Red Riding Hoods standing in various positions around the warehouse. The roar of the chain saw subsides. Carl holds the glass eyeballs over his own eyes and tilts his head mechanically from one side to the other. He laughs and snorts, feigning a limp.

My dear, what firm milky breasts you have, all the better to . . .

He pops the glass eyeball into his mouth, rolling it between his lips, which close over it like eyelids. Slowly he reaches for Sarah's throat and pulls the bow of her cloak so it falls off her shoulders onto the floor. Sarah squeals through tightly pressed lips.

For Christ's sake, Carl, she'll catch her death of cold, says the seamstress.

Carl and Sarah have been using a glue that foams into a cement. It has been taken off the market because the fumes are highly toxic, but over the years Carl has grown accustomed to using it and he knows a guy who imports it from Italy. It's a two-part solution and becomes active when the two separate solutions are mixed. Sarah and Carl are the only ones in the workshop. She's pouring the solution and he's holding the bucket for her. She spills the solution over his hands and frantically tries to wipe it. The foam has an acid base, and in her effort their hands have become stuck together. Carl shouts obscenities between his teeth and drags her to the sink. It's difficult for him to get at the cold water tap. Sarah is crying hysterically and his other hand is stuck to the bucket. It takes him fifteen minutes to separate their hands. The seamstress hears the commotion from the kitchen down the hall and gets the first aid kit. She wraps their hands with burn ointment and gauze. Carl apologizes for cursing at Sarah and sends her home. He stays a long time in the empty warehouse, his burnt hands cradled between his knees.

Haloes

A halo is the vibration of that which is perfect. Once the fish in the harbour of St. John's were so thick and silver they slowed sailing vessels. The great fire of 1892 razed the city when it became imperfect. Now sometimes, something is added, a hoar frost, a shipment of mangoes, fog, and the equation of the city can't contain its perfection. There's a surplus that you must stand very still to see. Perfection spills over in a glow at the edges of the city.

There's a photograph of the house my parents built together when it was just a skeleton. Blond two-by-fours like a rib cage around a lungful of sky. They worked back to back shifts in the restaurant they sold before I was born. The house was built on the weekends. I never once heard my parents make love, or saw them naked together. But the photograph of the two-by-fours is like walking in on them, unexpected. The house without its skin. Their life together raw, still to come.

I sat on the bar stool next to Philip. I can talk to Philip only when I'm drunk. I know things about him. He has a small daughter in Germany. He doesn't talk much. At the bar, I said to him, Now, Philip, how do you justify having a kid in Germany? Some poor young woman taking care of a baby all by herself? Philip barely moves his lips when he talks. There's a lisp like a run in a silk stocking. A ventriloquist throwing his voice into his own mouth.

He has that weird relationship with alcohol few people can maintain. He soaks himself in it every night without letting it own him. He's forty-six and liquor hasn't ruined his face. Instead of making him old, it's kept him from maturing, from ever making enough money to leave the city. He designs stained glass windows. I saw him in a church once, staring at his work, red and blue light floating over him like tropical fish; another face surfacing in his face, his true expression. There's something sexually magnetic about Philip's drinking, as if he could easily ignite.

His face turned crimson. I was giggling. We had been walking across a lake of clear alcohol, our fingertips barely touching, and suddenly lost belief in our buoyancy. I know a woman who left her house at two in the morning and knocked on Philip's door. He was watching television with a remote, the empty walls reflecting a syncopated beating, like butterfly wings. He had a plaid wool blanket wrapped around his knees. Whatever happened between them wasn't pleasant and she didn't say anything much about it. She said he had just finished an orange and two of his fingers were sticky, webbed together.

She separated his fingers with her tongue, tasting the orange pulp. This is a strange detail, but I have picked up a few esoteric things like this about Philip without even listening for them. He eats marmite. Once some teenagers lured him into an alley and beat him with pickets torn from a fence, breaking two of his ribs. When he's absolutely drunk he can sink every ball on a pool table. I asked about his daughter again, not making the connection between his red face and his rage.

Philip didn't raise his voice. He said, If you were a man I'd punch you in the face. What a stupid question. How can you ask something like that? If you don't get away from me I will punch your face in. You're a mother. I can't believe you're a mother. You haven't learned anything in your whole life.

I almost asked Philip to punch me. I willed it. A smack in the face would have evened things out, tipped me off the bar stool. I realized that over the previous ten years I had gathered only little splinters of Philip.

That afternoon I had been on the veranda with my daughter blowing psychedelic bubbles. The bubble solution was saturated with glycerine and that's what made the colour so lurid. Hot pink, chartreuse, turquoise. The bubbles trembled. One touched the splintery wood rail without breaking. My daughter and I, shadows stretching over the convex surfaces, bursting. I slid off the bar stool and went back to my seat before Philip decided to hit me. He stood up and pulled on his bomber jacket. It was grey nylon, and the wrinkles in its back seemed to shimmer a one hundred proof hatred as delicate as a bubble.

That night I dreamed I was about to take a penis in my mouth, but there was a jagged piece of glass embedded in it, and it split my lower lip. Blood gushed freely and I got weak, the same weakness that happens when you give blood. A beatific lightness that absolved me.

This incident with Philip was nothing. Something he probably wouldn't remember in the morning. But it sank inside me. It made me avoid the cafes and stores and streets where I thought I might run into him. It made me want to leave the city. Move away.

I'm reading one of the volumes of *The History of Haiku* that Gordon Austin left for me before he committed suicide. He was someone else whose pain I brushed up against accidentally. I knew him for only one night. We went on a blind date. He was an American, a draft dodger who manufactured false eyelashes in Ontario, a front to employ illegal immigrants, he said. Gordon had followed a woman to Newfoundland. He took me to an expensive restaurant, but he couldn't taste the food. Gordon had no sense of smell. He talked fast. I hardly said anything. The restaurant emptied. The waiters were leaning against the back wall waiting to go home. He kept talking. He said he was rich. He was working on sonar radar graphics, writing a program that could draw icebergs three-dimensionally for free floating oil rigs. You're only seeing the very tip, he said. His heart wasn't in it, though. He was thinking he'd buy a fast convertible, drive to Mexico. I could go if I wanted. He did buy the convertible shortly after our date, I heard. He bought it and left town for a month. Then he came back and left the haiku books for me in the restaurant where I was working, did a few other errands, and drove the silver convertible off Red Cliff. I couldn't understand why he had driven back to St. John's from Mexico to commit suicide. He had lived in St. John's for only the last five years of his life.

I read, "the haiku is like a finger pointing at the moon. It's important that it's not a bejewelled or perfect finger. It only points to something." I met Mike, my husband, after that. We were out drinking and Mike brought me home to his apartment, which was Gordon's old apartment. Mike had used the last of Gordon's shaving cream, wore a pair of Gordon's construction boots that were left under the bathroom sink. They fit him perfectly.

My mother's only sister, Sherry, is a real estate agent. The best in St. John's. In the weekend paper there's a whole page, a pyramid of real estate agents' photographs. Sherry is always at the top, or in the second line from the top. The agents are placed according to their sales. Sherry is afraid of two things. Fire and cats. She says when she was a baby, a cat lay over her face, filling her mouth and nose with fur, almost suffocating her. She was less than two years old but she remembers it. Cats are attracted to the smell of milk on the baby's breath. She didn't want Mike and me to buy this house. A fire trap, she said.

I was sewing a dress for my step-daughter with a friend who lives on the other side of the city. We were drinking coffee and Tia Maria. The phone rang and it was Mike. He said he

was standing in the front doorway of our house. Fire was pouring down the street. He said it was still safe there, but embers as
big as his fist were dropping at his feet. The sky is orange, he
said. I pulled the phone over to the window. There was an
orange and black cloud breathing in the sky on the other side
of the city. I said, That's over my house. He said, You should see
it, it's like lava in the street. They'll evacuate us when it gets hot
enough.

I ran home. Some streets were blocked. Ours was a frozen
river of water from the fire hoses. A blizzard of orange flakes.
I had to cover my head with my scarf to keep my hair from
catching fire. Mike had closed the front door because of the
soot and smoke. The radio said if the fire reached our street
the whole of downtown would be lost. It said the firemen were
losing control. There were high winds. A policeman rapped on
the door of our house with a billy knocker. He said, Move
now, NOW. The street was full of people carrying blankets,
photo albums, figurines. A spark landed on my daughter's hand,
making a tiny burn. We went to my sister's, stayed up all night
listening to the radio, drinking, unable to get drunk. At three in
the morning the radio said the firemen had contained it. Our
house was safe. I felt a quick stab of disappointment. I wasn't
comfortable in the city any more.

I woke early, afraid of looting. The Dominion supermarket
had burned to its foundation. Blackened girders twisted up
from the debris. Beautiful arcs of water shot from the fire trucks
at the four corners of the lot. Everything hissing, steaming, delicate rainbows. Under a broken metal shelf I saw a pile of

brilliant oranges, strangely preserved, each with a tiny white cap of snow. Our front door had been beaten in, tracks of soot over the carpet — the police had checked each house for someone left behind.

Since the fire the house has become infested with mice. The cat is playing with a mouse now, under my chair. I have my feet drawn up on the seat. I smash the mouse under a book. The cat finally bites its head. I hear the crunching of the bones of the mouse's skull between the cat's teeth; although the body is still moving, the tail has become a stiff S. In a few seconds the cat has devoured the entire body. She gives a cry. I half expect the mouse to scramble out of her mouth, whole. Perhaps because I know the mice will keep coming.

My daughter caught cold the night we were evacuated. Her cough sounds like cotton ripping. I draw her into me, her spine between my breasts, the soles of her feet burning against my thigh. I curl around her like a shell around a soft snail. Even her fingers are hot, as if the fire entered her hand through the little burn. When I was a child I used to climb into bed with my sister because I wanted to protect her from the devil. I believed the devil could draw my sister away through her dream, to a parallel universe, where there was a parallel city. Anything could be drawn out of this world, sucked into that one. Three years younger, she slept on her stomach. I'd put my nose in her hair. It had the colour and smell of unripe corn. She dreamed so strenuously that her cheeks were red, her lips slightly parted. I would lie on top of her, matching limb for limb, my arm over her arm, my leg over her leg, my fingers locked into hers.

The way you lie flat if someone has fallen through the ice. The devil couldn't pull us both down. I'd hook the bone of her ankle between my toes. I could stop her from falling too deeply that way, by hooking the bone of her ankle, but that always woke her up and she'd throw me off.

I went to see a Japanese performance artist. Wine glasses set in a circle like the numbers of a clock. Each wine glass filled with a different coloured spice. Grey-green, mustard, turmeric. He tipped the contents out on the floor and they floated down in gaseous clouds. On the video screen it looked like an aerial view of the Earth. The way the Earth looks as though it's made of water and cloud, with nothing holding it together. The video cameras were as fragile as cheap toys. He attached wires to himself, and a gas mask with a paper bag on the end, that filled and crumpled with his breathing. The screens showed a mushroom cloud exploding over and over, silently. Then he made a pyramid of the wine glasses and poured a jug of honey into them. The honey clung to the stems of the glasses until each glass was filled. It glistened in the spotlight, the whole pyramid one viscous city of glass. Then he put a syringe into his arm and poured his own blood into the glass, mixing it with his finger.

I became fascinated with real estate when Aunt Sherry became an agent. All of my cousins punctuated every emotional event by buying or selling a house. It took me a while to recognize this pattern. Who would expect symbolism in real estate? But when I think of it, Sherry has made real estate her life. There's her religion — a private part of her I can just barely guess the workings of — the fierce and protective love she has for her family, and real estate. I see all these parts of her bleed into each other. The houses she has bought and sold are spread out over the city like clues in a scavenger hunt. Some houses she's sold three and four times to different families, noting the changes in wallpaper, carpet, light fixtures, as though the house has a camouflage that matches the families that move in. She will often point out houses that have ghosts. A house where a son murdered his seventy-three-year-old mother, and she was found two weeks later. Sherry says this property is eternally on the market, the house like a lost soul that can't find bodies to move into it. She's bought houses for all her children, and when any of them tell a story, they always start, When we were on Holbrook Avenue, or Forest Road, or Prince of Wales Street.

There's a small island of trees and grass near my house. My daughter and I played there tonight, to bring down her fever. It had snowed the night before, covering the bone dry sidewalks, and another squall blew over in the afternoon. It was past Sarah's bed time, and my toes were cold in my rubber boots, but we stayed out as long as we could. The streetlights threw perfect shadows from the trunks of the trees, thick straight columns like the Parthenon's. An image drawn with sonar radar of a three-dimensional palace. I thought of Gordon Austin and his haiku books, of Philip's daughter playing in the snow of another continent. Sarah and I trampled the snow but the columns still looked clean, the shadow edges hard.

I imagine a map of the city with plastic inlays of Sherry's sales, family migration patterns from one neighbourhood to another. Each move changing lives irrevocably. Sherry is responsible for it. You sell a house to a customer and five years later they'll be back to you for another. There are only three things to think about in selling real estate. Location, Location, Location.

In India several years ago I was on a tour of a city palace. A guide separated me from the crowd, ushered me into a stone tower. Before I knew what was happening he had bolted the door and the windows. No light leaked in. The darkness seemed to affect my inner ear and I swayed. Before I could scream he struck a match. There were thousands of convex mirrors imbedded in the walls. The guide, myself and the flame — reflected, wobbling. The guide said, The bridal chambers, night of a thousand stars. Our image splintered infinitely. Smashed but contained whole in each of the convex mirrors.

Author's Acknowledgements

The author would like to thank the following institutions for their support: The Canada Council, Newfoundland and Labrador Arts Council, and St. John's City Arts Jury.

I am grateful to my editor, Beverley Daurio. Many thanks to all the writers in The Burning Rock for sharing their talents, particularly Stephanie Squires, Claire Wilkshire, Lawrence Mathews and Michael Winter. Thank you to Jane Urquhart and Edna Alford and Roger Greenwald for their support and criticism. For all their love and laughter I am forever grateful to Steve Crocker and my big and extended family. I would also like to say a big thank you to the gang at Anansi, especially Sarah MacLachlan, Martha Sharpe, Laura Repas, Matt Williams and Kevin Linder, for his fine eye.

"Wisdom Teeth" and "Meet Me in Sidi Ifni" were published in *Canadian Fiction Magazine*.

"Degrees of Nakedness" and "Ingrid Catching Snowflakes on Her Tongue" were published in *Prism International*.

"Nipple of Paradise" was aired on CBC National as well as published in *Coming Attractions* '94 with "Haloes" and "Purgatory's Wild Kingdom."

"Carmen Has Gonorrhoea" was published in *Extremities*, an anthology of fiction from The Burning Rock, Newfoundland.